# The Camel's Dead.

Timothy Conehead. .

The Invincible.

❤

ISBN: 0993107672
ISBN-13: 9780993107672

DEDICATION

This book is dedicated to the memory of Sir Lord Jack of the Kingdom of Goodness and Love who on 5th August 2016 aged 18 years took up residence at Rainbow Bridge, where he will be waiting for me to come and take him on a message. Also to all the other border collies I have rescued loved and lost, not forgetting those I still have. At the time of writing I still have Laddie the Baddie, Princess Freya the Hunter and of course Timothy Conehead the Invincible.

The dedication continues to all rescues whether centre based or online including, Dogs Trust with special thanks to Evesham Special needs unit, Freshfields Animal Rescue, Carla Lane Animals in Need, R.S,P,C.A. Liverpool, Protecting Preloved Border Collies, Lily's Border Collie Lifeline, Border Collie Rescue, Shamans Legacy Dog Rescue, Rescue Me Animal Sanctuary, Many Tears, The Freedom of Spirit Trust For Border Collies and The Border Collie Trust. All of the volunteers who help run these places and all the volunteer drivers who transport these lucky ones up, down and across the country.

You are all stars and I salute you.

Without some of the above I would not have had the sheer pleasure and joy of loving and 'correcting' so many beautiful collies and being loved and herded back in return.

Please support your local rescue centres or any of the many online rescues. No matter what breed you are after there will be a rescue centre with that breed in just waiting for your Love and to find their 'furever' home.

❤

If  you can't adopt then please
Foster, if you can't foster then please
Sponsor, if you can't sponsor then please
Volunteer, if you can't volunteer then please
Donate, if can't donate then please
Educate, if you cannot do this then please
Share posts on social media and cross post if you can.

All of the above saves lives, you could save a life today simply by 'liking' a post and you could save more by sharing it.
Remember..

All you need is Love ❤□ and Love is all you need.
Oh and a border collie or two or three or four..

Love,
Kathleen
❤

# ACKNOWLEDGMENTS

I've been privileged to own, foster and rehabilitate many border collies throughout my life but never had one quite as young as Timothy. He was nine months old and an emergency rescue who I intended to foster for a short while until a forever home could be found for him. I was told that the poor lad had been kept initially locked in a bathroom and later muzzled and locked in a car. At that time I had two old codgers Sir Lord Jack who was my top dog and aged 16 and Laddie the Baddie who was 14, the day before Timothy arrived on my doorstep I had welcomed Freya into my home, she had been used for breeding I had been informed and then cast out when her last litter produced only one pup. There are some cruel callous people in this world.

To say he was a handful is an understatement. The boy was wild and had zero social skills whatsoever and all the energy of a border collie pup. Oh my, I did wonder if I had bitten off more than I could chew.

I love writing and so I decided to keep an online diary of his antics and many people enjoyed them so I carried on. I decided that he was in training to my oldest and most precious boy Sir Lord Jack of the Kingdom of Goodness and Love who could do no wrong. Laddie the Baddie would teach him how to be naughty and Princess Freya the Hunter would help me to keep him in check.

I am often told that Timothy's tales are hilarious, they are certainly full of innuendo as he misunderstands just about everything and then misinforms everyone of whats going on in his new home at 'Kathleen's School of Correction.'

He plays with himself on the intersex, he wants to copulate like the bunnies and he is just plain and simply adorable. I did of course adopt him although he doesn't know this, he is told that when he has managed to be good for a whole month then we will review his foster status and see about adopting him.

I hope you enjoy reading Timothy's Tales as much as I have

enjoyed writing them and who knows there may even be a sequel.

If you do enjoy his diaries then please leave me feedback on Amazon and Facebook if you can.

# The Camel's Dead

by

Timothy Conehead

The Invincible.

❤

## Timmy Day Two.

31st March 2015

Down Timmy -

No Timmy -

Timmy come here -

Down Timmy - Timmy!

Timmy NO!

Timmy BE-HAVE!

Timmy STOP NOW!!

TIMMY!!!

Thank goodness for Freya that's what I say!

I left him downstairs in the crate last night as he isn't quite house-trained but not far of it I reckon. He cried for around twenty minutes and then settled down.

It's like having a hurricane in the house most of the time but he is a cutie.

He was clean last night and has had loads of OTT praise for relieving himself outside today, we had an hours run where he met a chihuahua who didn't really want to play with him but Timmy persuaded him otherwise!

He has now settled down and is fast asleep after driving me crackers during a webinar. Hey ho such is life.

## Day Three
## Wednesday April 1st.

Hello, My name is Timmy and I'm a nine month old Border Collie and I have come to Kathleen's house of correction to be taught some manners.

I think she likes me as she keeps saying 'just my luck' and 'what did I do to deserve this!' It's such fun.

I was locked up in my old house in a car so it's much better here as we go for big long runs only I have to keep going on a short lead because I have no manners, could someone send me some please?

Love Timmy. xx

## Day Four.

### Thursday 2nd April

Hello, Timmy here again!

I'm going to end up in big trouble, I thought it might be fun to have some sexytime  with Freya but she wasn't in the mood and she bit me and then my foster mummy shouted at me and I was put on a short lead again.

Jack and Laddie looked like they were laughing at me too, Just wait until mummy isn't looking.

We are going out for a steak sometime over the weekend, is that what a stake out is?

Love Timmy. xx

## Day Five
## Friday 3rd April.

Hello, Timmy reporting in!

It's Good Friday today and the good news is my foster mummy says I am now crate trained! Well I am in the house anyway. I love my food so much that each time she brings me out of my crate she tells me what a good boy I am and then fills the Kong ball back up with sweeties and puts it back in there and locks the crate up so every-time we go in that room I want to go in to get the sweeties but I can't because it's locked! So when it is time for me to go in there she opens it up and in I trot. I was invited to go for a drive with them all earlier though and I wouldn't go!

Oh I nearly forgot to tell you, mummy was cooking sausages for us yesterday and she had half of them in the pan and half of them on the worktop and so when she went to put something in the bin I ate the half that were still raw. She wasn't very pleased with me. She said I was as light as a leaf no that's not right - ah yes I know - she said I was a light fingered thief! I have a feeling that's not a good thing to be.

Love Timmy. xx

Day Six Saturday
4th April 2015

Here I am again, Timmy the hurricane!

I'm in trouble again. I tried to have sexy-time  with a really big German Shepherd and mummy wasn't pleased! She say's I won't be Timmy big balls for much longer, I'm not sure what she means but the German Shepherd called Storm didn't seem to mind fortunately for me the owner thought it was funny.

I missed it out yesterday but I have to tell you that I have been banned from my foster mummy's bedroom, I erm well I did a rather large messy smelly scooby doo poo on her plush lilac carpet and erm well, she wasn't very happy so I am banned for life! Or at least until I am properly house trained..

Becky and the daddy came today for lots of food and I helped! I supplied the wine, no I've got that wrong all I did was whine to get in to help mummy cook her fine dining dishes for Easter Saturday but she wouldn't let me.. Love Timmy. X

.

Day seven Easter
Sunday 5th April 2015

Hello, my name is Timothy and I'm a Border Collie, I've decided Timothy is much more fitting for special boy like me, however I am not having a good day. I have been sat on the naughty step nearly all day because my foster mummy has been cooking and she didn't like me helping her all the time. I have tried to have sexy time with everyone in the house today apart from mummy and I keep getting told off.

I'm a bit worried as I think mummy might have dementia or is she demented? I can't remember now..

Last night after dinner I discovered I really like port wine, it's really really nice !! I drank it when mummy went out of the room and Becky thought it was funny and didn't say anything so mummy poured another but she caught me drinking it! She wasn't very happy at all, apparently it's the good stuff and now I won't be getting any pocket money or any sweeties either. It's really confusing being a nine month old border collie.

All for now,
Love Timothy xx

Day eight Monday 6th April

Hello, my name is Timothy and I'm a sexy thing!

I've been good today as well as being naughty! When I first came to stay with my lovely foster mummy I didn't bring any manners with me and I didn't know what a pecking order was either. Sir Lord Jack gets fed first here and then Laddie the Baddie and then Princess Freya and then any one who might be sexy. [that's me in case you didn't guess it] anyway, when mummy put Jacks dinner in front of him on my first day I kind of lunged at it and ate it all before he or mummy could say OMG!

Anyway since then I've had to be in a straight jacket while I wait for the others and then I get my dinner. Well, today mummy had a spot of lunch and decided to let us all have a bit of her leftovers and first she gave some to Jack and then she gave some to Laddie and then Freya and then she looked at me who was sitting wagging my bum and smiling and looking sexy and being nice in the pecking order line and she said OMG again and she gave me an extra bit for being such a good boy and then I spoiled it all by wanting more sexy time with Freya who wasn't very happy with me!

At least I did one good thing and I know I can do that same good thing again to get some more treats and make mummy smile.

Love Timothy xx

Day nine Tuesday
7th April

Hello my name is Timothy and I'm a frustrated border collie.. It has been one whole day since my last confession and life isn't good.

I'm not allowed to mention the 'S' word today as I have been very naughty and Jack isn't happy with me at all and neither is my foster mummy! So I've decided to sing you all a little song by Right said Timothy..

'I'm too 'hmm hmm' for my coat, too hmm hmm' for my tail, too hmm hmm' for my collar - I'm too hmm hmm' for my legs, too hmm hmm' for my lead, too hmm hmm' by far!'

There, that feels better and I won't get told off now. I've been mostly naughty today with just a tiny bit of good I've been mostly incorrigible and also in the food cupboards. I think tomorrow we are having a steak out.

Love Timothy. xxxx
P.S. I'm enclosing a picture of Princess Freya wearing her very sexy mud boots, don't you think she is gorgeous? She had just returned from a pamper day at Dawn's and needed to cool down.

## Day ten
## Wednesday 8th April

Hello my name is Timothy and I'm a border collie and I am also a a star!!! It has been one day since my last confession.

It has been a week now since I did a big smelly steaming scooby doo poo in the house or watered anywhere indoors so it is official now, I am house trained!! The people from the Guinness book of records will be around to interview me soon, I like being a star.

We went for a steak out today only it wasn't quite what I expected! When we got to Buzzards Rest we stopped and mummy grabbed me by the throat and drove a stake through my heart and kept me pinned down to the ground for three hours!!!

Only joking!!!

Mummy put a stake in the ground and attached my long line to it, then she let the others wander off and ignored me and then we did 'in tents' training and every time I started to wander off she called me and enticed me with treats! It was good fun. It's such hard work living here.

Love Timothy xx

## Day twelve Friday 10th April,
## Ladies Day.

Hello my name is Timothy and I'm a brave border collie. I nearly died again today – twice! It has been tow days since my last confession.

My foster mummy's smart phone broke last night and although the world didn't end she needed to get it fixed quick. This meant we all had to go on a message! Jack jumped in first, he gets the whole of the back seat to himself, we think he must be royalty. Then Laddie and Freya jumped in the back well Laddie has to have his bum lifted up, then mummy looked at me and I slinked away but she come and picked me up again and put me in the back, I was scared again but I tried to be brave. She took us to the Virgin shop and I thought I was going to get a surprise but they said she had to go to the apple shop instead. I was a really good boy just sitting in the back and when we got home we all sat and stayed while the back door was opened and we all got a treat. She says that by the time she is finished with me I will be jumping in by myself!

Later on we went out and we met Max who is a very, very big German Shepherd, a failed police dog. He is a bit older than me and six times bigger and nearly flattened me and I thought I was a gonner. Max was with his owner and his three grandchildren who were 5, 6 and 7 and we all played with the grandchildren - all of us and we've decided we all like grandchildren and we think they were fun and they all thought we were fun too!
I'm just exhausted with all this growing up and being brave, but it is fun.
Love Timothy. xx

## Day thirteen,Grand National Saturday
## 11th April 2015

Hello I'm Timothy and I'm still a border collie. This is my confession for today.

Oh it's been such a hectic day today. Remember when I arrived with no manners and ate everything I could first without asking? Well, I have had to be locked in one room while Jack gets his dinner, then Laddie and then Freya and lastly the little 'hmm hmm' thing, that's me.

Anyway, this morning I must have looked like I might be behaving myself just a bit and mummy made me sit and stay and then she fed Sir Jack and then Laddie and then Freya and I was still sitting and polishing the floor with my tail and then she fed me! How cool is that? And, and we did the same thing tonight too, I can't be trusted in the kitchen by myself yet but I am practicing to be a superstar everyday.

Disaster followed breakfast though as we had to go on another message but I was very good again sitting nicely and trying to look brave and not making a single sound and I've started breathing again too, as we get let out again after we've done a stay when the door opens, mummy say's I will get to like it one day...

Today we met those grandchildren again, none of us have ever been grandchildren tested before, not properly we've just never come across any and we all passed with flying colours! We played with them for ages and we are hoping to see them again very soon.

Mummy is having port tonight and I keep trying to have a taste but she won't let me near her glass, just wait until she goes to the loo.....
Speak soon,
Love Timothy xx

Day fifteen -
Monday 13th April 2015.

Hello my name is Timothy and I'm a border collie - please send HELP immediately!It is the end of the world!!

Can you send for the Royal Marines and the SAS and the air ambulance and anyone else who can help!!

We had to go on a message this morning without having had any breakfast or anything, I was so cool as I jumped into the car all by myself! Then we got to this place and I was abandoned there and it was terrible! There were green men everywhere and they all took turns to stab me with needles! I couldn't get away. They had me pinned down with bayonets and they came at me with machetes and dissected me and mutilated me and removed very precious jewels that belonged to me and no one else and I can't cope and I need a lawyer and the police! Yes call the police too and MI5 and the European courts of humane rights as well!

As soon as I woke up I started talking to them and demanding my rights! They just thought it was funny that I was a talking dog and didn't take any notice of what I said! Then mummy came and it was ok again and I met her friend Jo with the dodgy pussy and then they put the cone of shame on my head, I am so depressed all I do is stare at the floor I am just so sad.

I'm sure I will never recover from this...
Love Timothy. xxxx

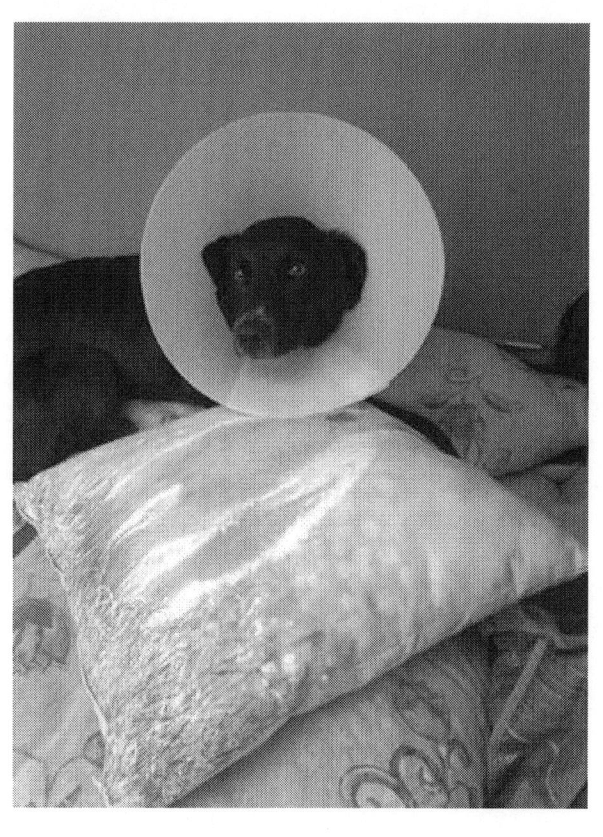

❤

Day sixteen Tuesday
14th April 2015.

My name is Timothy and I am Cone Head The Magnificent! It has been one day since my last confession and nothing keeps me down.

Hello,

I can run like the wind and soar like an eagle but I can't find my crown jewels! I can cause mayhem wherever I go though and I'm enjoying upsetting everyone. I just hold my head up and run and I manage to get whoever is standing in my way, it's great fun. I know Jack and Laddie are laughing at me but I'm getting my own back as Cone Head the Magnificent!!!

I was told last night by my very good friends Simba and Harry that my crown jewels have been removed to lower my toblerone levels, life is so confusing, I thought we weren't allowed chocolate oh how can my chocolate levels be lowered by mutilating me with bayonets and machetes.. I need to find some comfort and a lawyer.
I will keep you informed.
Love Timothy. xxxx

Day seventeen Wednesday
15th April 2015

Anniversary of Hillsborough.
JFT96 YNWA.

Hello, my name is Timothy and I am Cone Head the Invincible, feared by everyone I meet! It has been one day since my last confession from Kathleen's House of Correction.

My toblerone levels are all over the place at the moment and Freya keeps examining my sweetbreads to check on their progress. I am having fun battering everyone with my cone and I have been assured I can still have sexytime in the future!

My good friend Simba is now a fully qualified scarecrow dog and available for hire for weddings, funerals and children's birthday parties.

Mummy's top of the range receptionist Jan has sent us a lovely present, I reckon it's all for me really - anyway there are lots of lovely treats, lots and lots and if mummy forgets to put them up high, well - a nod is as good as a wink to an invincible border collie..

Will let you know how they taste tomorrow.
Love Timothy xxxx

Day 19
Friday 19th April 2015.

Hello everyone! Timothy calling. AKA CONE HEAD THE INVINCIBLE!! It has been two whole days since my last confession I couldn't log on yesterday I'm afraid.

I'm really sorry about yesterday, Freya locked me in the basement - she is such a bully! There is no desktop or laptop down there and my smart phone and iPad just couldn't pick up a signal. Anyway, I managed to get out again and I  she loves me really but you know what women are like.

I went to see the green people today who mutilated me last week, I think my green lady is called uli and she loves me and would take me to live with her but her working hours are too long for an upwardly mobile young man such as I am but she thinks she might know someone who can accommodate my many and extravagant needs!

My tummy was a bit off yesterday so I have to take some more medicine, all will be well soon.

Mummy isn't feeling too good today and she might just have to disappear for a bit but if she does all will be well and we will look after her and get her back soon, we will do our best to keep her here though.
I'll keep you informed.
Love Timothy. xxxxx

Day Twenty five
24th April 2015 .❤

Hello Everyone, it's me Timothy Super Cone Head the Invincible and I'm a border collie. It has been five days since my last confession and I am free!!

I'm too sexy for my cone! I am pleased to announce that I have had my cone surgically removed and replaced with an invisible one!

The vet said that now my rectum is disappearing I can go back to do anything else I might fancy doing...

So today I have had sexy time with Freya and sexy time with Hogan and sexy time with Max and I've been getting told off by everyone and apparently there is this nice new food call bromide and I'm getting some very soon!

I am such a lucky boy and not to mention sexy too and I am so good just sitting nicely in the back of our chariot. I jump in there quite happily now and I'm beginning to enjoy our daily messages and every time the door gets open I sit nice and wait until I'm called to get out. I'm just so cool....

Love Timothy. xxxx

Day twenty seven
26th April 2016

My name is Timothy Conehead the Invincible, the unstoppable, the magnificent and I am a border collie. It has been two days since my last confession.

Erm, hello I've erm been just a bit naughty today and now I'm in handcuffs in the naughty drawer.

We went to the beach today and mummy said I was a nightmare and I'm not allowed back until my manners have improved! I wanted the statue to play with me and our Freya wanted it to throw her ball for her. Sir Jack and Laddie the baddie both laughed at us, they reckon we are a bit thick. Hark at Laddie, he thinks the microwave contains aliens which are about to attack us. Sheesh...

Anyway so anyway mummy was cooking liver and she forgot about me just for a minute as I have been so good lately and gorgeous and she just went to lay the table for lunch and while she wasn't looking I just couldn't help noticing this lovely big piece of liver looking all lonely in the pan and so I quickly rescued it , oh it tasted lovely your honour and I'm sure it was grateful to me for rescuing it only it was the piece that mummy was saving for her lunch and she wasn't pleased that I had rescued it at all so erm now you know why i'm in handcuffs in the naughty drawer. Sir Lord Jack reckons I'm here for at least ten years or until it's time to go on walkies again....
Love Timothy. Xxxx

My name is Timmy
and I stole a big
peice of liver out
of the pan...
I have been grounded
for a week.....

❤

Day Twenty Eight.
Monday 27th April 2015

My name is Timothy Conehead the Invincible, the unstoppable, the magnificent, the poorly sick hero! I am a border collie and it has been one day since my last confession.

Hello everybody, I had an accident last night and when my foster mummy came in and found it I just lied down on the floor and waited for her to shout and me and smack me I closed my eyes and waited for the smack but  she didn't.  She just looked at me with that 'Do it again Conehead and your dead meat' look that she has and just cleaned it up.

We went in the chariot then to see Uli the vet next who I think is in love with me and wishes she could have me always and forever to live with her and to adore me but she is too busy, so she just stuck a needle into me and Freya instead.  As we waited in reception for our ration books, no that's not right oh sorry we waited for our identity cards!  Then it wasn't my fault but I had diarrhoea all over the reception floor, oh it was awful but everyone was very kind and very nice to us and when I got home I had projectile vomiting too!  I was just going to say I was sick but doesn't projectile vomiting sound dead boss?

Anyway so anyway the diarrhoea decided to be friends with me for a while and it wasn't very nice at all but mummy didn't shout at me not once your honour, she just cuddled me and said it would be gone soon.

I had to be restrained on a lead because mummy said it was best not to jump up and down too much when my tummy was not very happy. She gave me some bung up pills, three grains of rice and a sliver of chicken for dinner and is hopeful that my belly will be more friendly tomorrow.

Mummy is having intercourse all over the spiders web again tomorrow morning and we have lots of messages to go on so we are all having an early night to reserve some energy.

Sir Lord Jack who can do no wrong is just so distinguished and I am in training to him and he is trying to teach me how to be perfect and do no wrong too so that one day I can have the back seat of the chariot all to myself.
I will write again as soon as I can.

Love Timothy xxxx ❤

Day twenty nine
Tuesday 28th April 2015.

My name is Timothy Conehead the Invincible the unstoppable, the Magnificent and I have been naughty again. It has been one day since my last confession.

Oh it's been a busy day here, we had to get up early to go for a run and then mummy went on a message and didn't take us with her so while she was out I found a pair of her gloves. There was a bow thing on there but I decided it looked like a spider toy and so I chewed it until I had chewed one of its legs off! It wasn't on the floor but she hadn't put it very high up on the shelf and I have very very long legs and can reach up higher than the others and well as I say your honour it looked just like a spider toy to me that was calling to be played with.

When mummy returned and she did notice the said spider toy languishing on the floor she looked at me with one of those looks that would turn the sun into a pillar of salt and I did tremble inside.

Anyway, I'm attaching exhibit one, mummy said that gloves are meant to be worn and so she did make me wear the offending gloves on my nose for ten hours while the others just laughed at me. I'm hoping that she hasn't noticed that I've chewed the metal fastener bit off the side of one of her black Hunter wellies. I suspect she will be just grateful that I only chewed the metal bit and I am certain she will be really pleased that I am helping her to be more tidy.

I nearly forgot to tell you, while she was hare coursing on the intercom the lecturer was just asking mummy a question and then the phone rang and then the other phone rang and our Freya started howling and I did join in too and mummy couldn't hear what he was saying, oh it was so funny. Mummy is going to unplug the phones in time for the next lecture.
Love Timothy xx xx

Day twenty nine
29th April 2015

My name is Timothy Conehead the Invincible and I'm a Border Collie. I have to confess I have been naughty again. It has only been one day since my last confession.

Well, really speaking I have mostly been good today apart from when I have been naughty. I am so clever I have managed to destroy an indestructible toy only mummy wasn't too happy about it. The shop people said that she has it it for more than a month and it can't be returned so mummy went like this, she went ' I'd just like a little word in your shell like, two words to be precise 'Trading Standards' so now it is being replaced for free and they are sending two of them as an apology. I don't feel nearly so bad about breaking it now and I have more to look forward to!
I've been on the rob again your honour and have an upset tummy to

prove it. I've had to write out one thousand and forty lines today saying ' I must never steal liver ever again or even for longer' It just tastes so nice but my tummy doesn't agree with my mouth.

Did you know that mummy works in a dead posh street? No, not Coronation Street silly, she works in Rodney Street and it's the Harley Street of the north which is also posh. Anyway, because it is posh or because it is so dead old the buildings are listing at grade two and lots of film companies do come to do filming there. Well it is so exciting and they are filming again this week and we were thinking that if mummy took us into work with her then Jan, who is the number one top of the range cream of the crop dead boss receptionist might like to mind us all. We thought that Peaky Blinder might just want to have four gorgeously handsome border collies to be his minders and we thought if we just popped outside to see a dog about a man while they were filming then we might just get discovered! Mummy said to dream on, I think that means we need to sleep on it.
Love Timothy. xxxx

Day thirty.
Thursday 29th April 2016

My name is Timothy Conehead the Invincible and I'm a border collie and I've been grassed up! Just one day has passed since my last confession.

Hello everyone, mummy has been wondering what I have been doing with my cone hoovering the ground as I go but she is too busy thinking things like wondering why she has four naughty collies and things like that, oh no sorry. Sir Lord Jack is never naughty, Sir Lord Jack can do no wrong, Sir Lord Jack has balls of gold and is training me to be perfect in every-way too. Mummy looks at me with that scary look and she goes like this 'Conehead you are a grasshopper and you have a lot to learn from my special boy, best you learn it quick before you get squished like a grasshopper.' I didn't know I was a grasshopper I thought I was a border collie.

Anyway so anyway where was I oh yes Simba's mum Anne who is mummy's friend has grassed on me and mummy has now noticed your honour that I quite like eating poo!

She went like this 'it's twenty five years in the cellar for you Conehead and that's after I'll  put a steak through your heart and ground you for a week!' I think that's what she said, I don't think she knows what to do really.

Anyway, I've been dead boss in the pecking order and I'm learning how to be dead grown up like the big boys, don't you think I am adorable and sexy as well as being dead boss?
Speak soon,
Love Timothy xxxx

9th May 2015

My name is Timothy Cone-Head the Invincible and I'm a border collie I am also a coprophiliac. It has been nine whole days since my last confession.

Hello everyone, I'm really sorry I haven't been keeping my diaries up, we've been on a nine day bender.

It's been terrible here, I think it was Jan's fault, she's mummy's top of the range receptionist and she has been starring in a porno film they are making on Rodney Street! Jacks eyes are rolling again I must have something wrong, oh that's right Laddie says it's a promo film not a porno film - they don't look much different to me and I'm sure Jan could star in both of them. I'm going to meet her soon and we're going to be shooting people and taking photographs!

It's all very exciting here there is so much going on and there have been erections everywhere you look and now a lot of them are deflated and not very happy. Anyway, mummy say's I have to get some training in and get a job as I won't be getting any benefits from Mr Condom the pig lover and I'm trying really really hard and today I ran upstairs to tell her her alarm had gone off on her iPhone and mummy said I could be a hearing dog for the blind and - oh whats wrong now?

Sir Lord Jack has just rolled his eyes at me again and Laddie and Freya are too busy laughing and they won't tell me what I've said wrong. Just wait until I'm famous, they won't be laughing then.

Anyway listen, we've been on a secret mission while mummy was on the game and we've been sending secret agent Laddie down to the bowels to try to find the secret that everyone is looking for but no luck yet.

Must go now, it looks like mummy is starting to come round, now where did I leave the bottle of port.....
Love Timothy. X

10th May 2015.

My name is Timothy Conehead the Invincible and I'm a border collie. One day has passed since my last confession.

Life at Kathleen's house of correction is deteriorating badly. We've been trying all day to get her out of bed to feed us but she won't move. I think she is dreaming of the next erection and I don't think she is very amused to it will be five years until she see's another erection. We're hoping we can find her a local erection just to keep her going. Or does anyone else know how we can get her another erection sooner please?

Sir Lord Jack of the Kingdom of Love has done some shopping on the intersex and has bought me a present, he has bought me my very own skate board, he say's when I have mastered this one he will let me have his super duper one from the loft! He says I have to get a move on as I am going to be in charge of transportation soon..

I have to go now as we are going to try and get mummy up again to feed us before we waste away to nothing and die an excruciating painful and violent death with our ribs sticking out and our innards nothing more than a faint distant memory, a bit like the erection mummy keeps dreaming about really.

I will keep you informed.

Love Timothy xxxx

11th May 2015 I

My name is Timothy Conehead the Invincible, I am a border collie and I'm still a coprophiliac. I have lost count of how many days I have been in Kathleen's correctional unit.

Mummy had a dream about poo last night and so did I! I like eating poo as often as I can. Somebody told her to add pineapple chunks to my meals and it will stop me but surprise surprise as our Cilla would say I still like poo!

Mummy says she is going to book me in to see me in work and I will be hypnotherapized and I won't want to eat poo anymore then, I think she is a spoil sport because I like eating poo.

I played with Max today, he is a big German boy, he's going to be having his sexy bits removed soon too. Max is very big and plays rough but I am not scared of him, I am Conehead the Invincible! Must go, I have skateboard practice to fit in before bedtime.

All for now,
Love Timothy xxxx

17th May 2015.

My name is Timothy Conehead the Invincible and I'm a border collie. It has been seven days since my last confession.

It's not good news I'm afraid. I have now destroyed all the toys that have lived here for years. I think we are needing an emergency fund-raising Conehead Aid concert or something similar as my foster mummy can't keep up with me and she now has dementia! No that's not right, Sir Lord Jack says I have her made her demented. I have managed to destroy every destructible toy and now I am working on the indestructible ones. The aforementioned toys your honour have lived here for years and years and years and some are family heirlooms. Our Freya had a lovely pair of squeaky flip flops that she brought here with her but not anymore thanks to Conehead the Invincible! All the fluffy toys have disappeared somewhere but not before I had destroyed Tigger, Elmo, Woody, The Cookie monster, and Jessie along with a few random bunnies and pussy's! I don't think mummy liked the rooms looking like they were covered in snow all the time.

While mummy was in the bath today I found loads of our bones and bits of my toys all sitting together in a basket so I arranged them nicely all over the floor for her in pretty patterns, mummy likes pretty patterns. Anyway so when she came down she went a funny colour and started sobbing uncontrollably and then started shouting 'Curtains! Curtains! That's it Timothy you are curtains!

I'm hoping she is going to buy me some red curtains to go with my new red collar.

It's not my fault I am still teething is it? I just need to chew everything, mummy has bought me an octopus who looks like Mr Snuffleupagus, I wonder how long he will last.?

Love Timothy. xxxx

## 21st May 2015

My name is Timothy Conehead the Invincible and I'm a border collie. It has been four days since my last confession your honour and I have really bad news. The camels dead!

It has been really dark her for a while but we are good at making mummy smile.

Anyway where was I? Oh I know my foster mummy has been tidying up and some of my favourite bones keep going missing and so anyway I had this tasty bone that I had been saving for ages and ages since last week and I was looking for a safe place to keep it and I found one! Her wellies were just sitting there where they don't belong and I thought 'I know I'll just keep my favorite bone in there so as it can become a vintage antique bone and taste lovely' I was sure that mummy wouldn't be wearing them for ages and ages and ages so I did it. I was really pleased to have found such a safe place.

There was one small tiny problem about to happen as it unfortunately rained in the nighttime your honour and I had forgotten all about my safe place by the time the morning came. We were all so excited about going out,. Mummy started putting her wellies on and even though Sir Lord Jack knew it was there he didn't say anything and all of a sudden there was a deathly blood curdling scream and blood everywhere and the paramedics had to come to remove her foot from my bone and that's it!! The camels dead! It's the final straw and the camels back is broken and that's an end to everything!

I didn't know we had a camel and I don't know where we keep him. He's in big trouble now though, I didn't see any straws either you know, I wonder how many humps our camels has? I'd like to go for a ride on a camel and camp in the desert and play tuggy with our Freya and sleep in an Arabian tent with the golden oldies!
I wonder if we keep our camel in the cellar or if we keep him in the bowels of Belles Haven I might go on an adventure and look.
Not just yet though, I am in hiding in the naughty drawer, I put myself there. I thought it was best to as I could see the machete cupboard was open.

I'll post again soon.
Love Timothy xxxx

23rd May 2015.

My name is Timothy Conehead the Invincible and I'm a Border Collie. It has been two days since my last confession and and I have an Aunty Pauline!

Hello,
Did you know I had an Aunty Pauline? She's a really very very nice aunty Pauline who I like a lot. She has brought me lots and lots and lots of teething toys to kill and I don't know where to start !
They're all mine and just for me and none of them are for Sir Lord Jack or Freya or Baddie or er I mean Laddie. They're all mine and I am so happy and excited and thrilled as I haven't had anything decent to play with for months and months and days and now I have dozens of my very own toys to hide and kill and chew oh and

I'm just so excited!

It feels like Nirvana and Heaven and Paradise and I am on cloud nine!

I've just realised they are nearly all tuggy toys so I will have to share with Our Freya after all, oh well. No doubt the golden oldies will be rolling their eyes at us if we play too rough.

I wonder if I have any more aunties waiting to shower me with gifts?

I will let you know if I do, all for now.
Love Timothy. xxxx

Day 55 Sunday
24th May 2015.

My name is Timothy Conehead the Invincible and I'm a border collie. It has been one day since my last confession and the responsible adult is missing.

Hello, Timothy calling! Yes, that's me the Invincible border collie. Can you help us please? We don't know where mummy is. It's a transvestite that we have been left on our own all day. We haven't been fed for days and days and days and at least since this morning.

Laddie says this happens every time the ships are in, apparently she has lots of friends on these ships and they give her and her friends lots of presents and money to buy special things. They are always pleased to mummy and her friends who can be out of the game for days on end while we are just neglected and hungry as we languish away just hoping she may return one day. I am not sure whether that should say 'out of the game' or 'out on the game' I am also not sure your honour if there is a big difference.

Sir Lord Jack is rolling his eyes around the room at me again he says I'm getting carried away by the fairies and I need to get my fiction right or he will have to take over. Did you know that there are fairies that live on Belles Haven? You have to be really special to be able to see them and sometimes they come to play with the unicorns in Unicorn Woods and Sir Lord Jack says that if I am very good he might take me to see them one day! I'm not sure I am ever going to be really good enough for Sir Lord Jack but I keep trying really really hard.

I played with Hogan today, I don't know what he is but he is a really really big boy but I soon sorted him out and his daddy was really pleased with me and gave me a sweetie, I don't think he noticed we didn't have the responsible adult with is. I hope she comes back soon.
Love Timothy xxxx x

Monday 26th May 2015
Day 56

My name is Timothy and I'm a Border Collie it has been two days since my last confession and the Booze Ships are in!

We need your help, does anyone know where our responsible adult is please? We still can't find her and we have heard that the booze ships are in, all three of them and we think they may be detaining our mummy against her free will.

We think she may have come home last night at some point, there are a big pile of bones that have been scattered around downstairs but no sign of anyone responsible not even mummy.

We can't get the TV to work but we have managed to get the intersex on so we are weaving away on the web.

I really wish Lord Sir Jack wouldn't keep rolling his eyes around or a big grey herring might just fly down one day and take those big eyes to feed to her baby herrings in the nest!

Anyway, I've been looking for some really snazzy coats on Easylay. Did you know that when I arrived I had a coat in my suitcase but it didn't work it was broken. Mummy said she would buy me a new one so I'm sure she won't mind me just looking at these lovely red ones, they will go with our new red collars and leads. I like the look of the red dickie bows too and now I'm looking at some new toys.

I've ordered some toys for all of us because I think our Freya and the golden oldies deserve some new toys and I've ordered some special puppy toys and now I think we should look for some adult toys for mummy.

I think I may have found where mummy bought her handcuffs from, hmm I'm looking at a rampant rabbit now and I'm thinking that it could be something that we could all have fun chasing but I thought they were all brown? I'll order a nice purple one, mummy likes purple.
If anyone sees the responsible adult please send her home..

I will write again soon.
Love Timothy. xxxx

Tuesday 27$^{th}$ May 2015
Day 58

My name is Timothy Conehead the Invincible and I'm a border collie. It has only been one day since my last confession and there are dead bodies everywhere..

Hello, there is blue murder here and I'm in hiding and fearful for my life and whether I will be fed in the morning. Mummy has found something decrepit going on in her playful account and is calling in the busies! It's terrible the house is filthy, no I mean it is crawling with the filth and I have to be away on my toes soon in case they spot me.

Oh no, Sir Lord Jack says the special branch are being called in and apparently there is a special department that deals only with the illegal buying of adult toys on the intercourse. It's just blue murder and people are dying all over the place and heads keep rolling 'and will continue to roll young Conehead!'

It's like a war-zone and I'm just hiding in the naughty drawer with my favourite vintage bone and my pink flamingo that my new aunty Pauline bought me, I am just too scared to come out! I was going to elope with Freya on our camel but I can't find it anywhere !

Can they take paw prints do you think? Or nail prints? I know I'll book myself in for a pedicure with Dawn, if I get my nails clipped they won't be able to pin it on me, will they?

I think I'll just keep my head down in the naughty drawer until the filth have cleaned up..

I'll write again soon,
Love Timothy xxxx

May 29th 2015
Day 60

My name is Timothy Conehead the invincible it has been only two days since my last confession and I've murdered the pink flamingo!

Hello Everyone,
I'm in big trouble again, my brand new pink flamingo that me newly acquired aunty Pauline bought for me has died! It's innards are scattered across mummy's axminster and she doesn't look very happy at all!

She has turned a sort of red colour and there is mist coming out of her ears and she looks really rather cross with me. I think I might just saunter out and hope she doesn't see me sauntering away..

I'm outside now with Sir Lord Jack and he says I am going to be posted back to Elaine in a plain brown parcel for sure now, only if she has enough stamps though because I am getting bigger by the day.

We are just casually looking through the window and hoping mummy has enough brandy in that cup of tea to calm her nerves and we've just sent Freya in with a tub of valium to just randomly place them next to her cup.

It's all quiet now and I think I may have got away with it so I am just playing with myself while I can.

Then she goes like this in a big loud voice, "Timothy Conehead come here this very minute immediately now!!"

Ooops, I think I might be in trouble again. "There is flock all over my carpet and I am not very pleased with you young man and if there is anymore flocking flock on my flocking carpets or any of my flocking floors then your flocking innards are going to be impaled on flocking railings which I will have specially installed to warn others about buying you flocking toys filled with flock! Do you understand young man? Do I make myself clear??"

I smiled in an innocent handsome sort of way and then gave mummy the nice smelly bone I had brought in to surprise her with. I think it did the trick though, she was lying on the floor laughing and crying for ever such a longtime after. I was very shocked at the amount of flocking that was going on though. I didn't know mummy was bi-sexual or should that be bi-lingual? Anyway I must remember to smile nicely for mummy when she decapitates me for her special railings. What does decapitate mean?
More soon,
Love Timothy. xxxx

Monday 1st June 2015

Day 63

My name is Timothy Conehead the Invincible and I'm a border collie. It has been three days since my last confession.

Hello everybody,

Do you remember me telling you about our lovely new red coats , the ones that the nice postman Les brought for us? You know, the postman who likes me and thinks I am adorable ?

Well so anyway mummy has a nice red coat too, I think she has a few nice red coats but some are for work and some are for walks. So where was I? Oh yes swinging from the banister. Mummy has this red coat that she keeps on the banister at the bottom of the stairs and she just leaves it there. When she goes out she puts food in one of the pockets and it's for training. Now Sir Lord Jack tells me that normally they don't get many treats here which is the only reason why they are being so nice to me!

Consequently and because of this the golden oldies have suddenly remembered that they know what 'touch' is and so they keep touching mummy's hand with their noses and sometimes a treat falls out into their mouths! They used to do this hundreds of years ago when they were young and that's all they have to do to get a treat is to just touch mummys hand! I have to do all kinds! I have to run all the way back to her and sit and smile in a sexy way I have to do a sit and stay, still looking sexy obviously. Sometimes I might have to think for myself what I can do to get a treat off mummy so I might bring a toy but it mightn't be the right toy to get a treat so I might bring another one to her and hope that this one might be the magic toy to get a treat for.

Anyway so anyway, somebody digressed me when I wasn't expecting it. So, mummy was kerb crawling on the web again and so I just thought I might just go and have a look at this red jacket to see if it was ok and everything and so I did.

When I got there I just pushed my nose into a pocket and it was 'the' pocket and there I was taking ecstasy and before I knew it I was in the land of Nirvana and Utopia and Heaven and Paradise and the Land of the White Light and everything and anyway I was just enjoying myself so much and having fun and then it happened.

“TIMOTHY! COME HERE THIS MOMENT YOUNG MAN!!” And I just froze, like Hans solo in Return of the Jedi, the bit with Jabba the Hutt. 'If only I had my light saber' I thought. I gently eased my nose out of the Nirvana pocket and did a very sexy looking sit stay with a totally innocent smile on my face.

Mummy went like this, she went “Timothy Conehead why are you so naughty” I was about to answer but Sir Lord Jack said it was a rectal question and to keep quiet and so I did.

She went “Timothy Conehead it is the cellar for you for six days” I slid away and hoped she hadn't noticed the letter I had written and had left on the hall table.

I'll write again soon,
Love Timothy. xxxx
.

Sunday 7th June 2015
Day 69

My name is Timothy Conehead the Invincible and it has been one week since my last confession and mummy has a new red Tshirt.

Mummy likes red and we all like red as we all have matching red things and this week mummy bought a new red t shirt and we all modelled our new red things together in the garden. Her red T shirt matches our red coats and leads and collars and even our identity tags are red. They are red hearts and mine says on it 'Timothy Conehead the Invincible ' Mummy says that she really hopes I don't get lost because she won't be owning up to knowing anyone called Conehead! I think I'd better be good and not get lost.

Did you know mummy was a pole dancer?

Well you see it is mummy's birthday on the 4th of June and well we've been badly neglected while she has been busy dancing on a pole celebrating her birthday before she might be getting sent down for a misdemeanor in the red light district of Liverpool!

Laddie the Baddie says it's her third offense and they will be throwing books at her while she is pole vaulting in the docks! Sir Lord Jack say's it will be ok as she has a magistrate in her pocket and if they do throw books we'll just get some more bookcases. I think that sounds like a very strange place to keep a magistrate your honour, she must have really big pockets, I wonder which red coat it is?

Mummy is upstairs and she's just gone like this, she went "Timothy Conehead you're not on my laptop again are you? I've decided it is another one of those rectal questions that don't need answering. Now she's just gone "Timothy, I don't want to find my secrets all over the intersex when I log on later you know. These people think I'm a respectable business woman."

Sir Lord Jack has just rolled his eyes at me again and Laddie giggled. Our Freya just walked out in disgust, I think she is just jealous because she can't type like me.
Anyway I'm going to speak to the nice postman tomorrow, the one who brings all the parcels in their plain brown packaging for mummy. I'm going to ask him if he knows what is in them...

I'll post again as soon as I can,
Love Timothy. xxxx
P.S. I am enclosing a picture of Laddie the Baddie, he was helping mummy out and being a waiter at her dinner party.

❤

Tuesday 9th June 2015
Day 71

My name is Timothy Conehead and I'm a border collie, it has been two days since my last confession and I'm a daddy!

So you see there is this chick from Essex and her name is Annie and she is really quite sexy and of course she fancies me as all the chicks do and so anyway we do the business and have a sexy-time and that's it! Or so I thought but then I was evacuated to Liverpool to this crazy place called Kathleen's School of Correction to be corrected and then today I am just playing with myself on the intersex and there she was as plain as the black eye I gave Freya this morning. It was Annie and she was just looking cute and sexy only now she's up the duff and she lives with mummy's friend.

So anyway I think it's best to say nothing like all responsible men would after a bit of hows your father and a nod's as good as a wink to a blind camel that may be living in the basement.

I'll be in deep smelly stuff if mummy discovers my faux paw and starts wanting to do maternity tests and blood and gut testing and I'm sure it wasn't me your honour as I'm sure I was wearing a poppadom while I was jiggy jigging and having a sexy-time.

I'll just delete the picture showing this impostor with her four sprogs, they can't possibly be mine as none of them are nearly as handsome as me. Please don't tell mummy that they might be or I'll be shot at dawn and then get hard labour in the cellar for ten years again.
I will send more information soon,
Love Timothy. xxxx

13th June 2015
Day 75

My name is Timothy Conehead the Invincible, it has been four days since my last confession and I need to confess again today that I have six Love puppies!!!

Mummy read my last post and she unceremoniously removed my blood and guts and sent it off to the benefits people and the thing is they can't rule me out as the daddy!! I am just going to take it on the shin bone and stand up like a man and admit I have six love puppies your eminence.

I say six love puppies, I suppose what I mean is I was in Love with Annie while we both enjoyed jiggy jigging but then as soon as she released my prized possession from her clutches after having it in lock down for a while I was spirited away to this strange place in Liverpool. Otherwise I would have hung around for more and done my civic duty your honour.

Anyway even though I was wearing a poppadom which doesn't seem to have been working I still had to be newted or sprayed just in case and, oh hang on. Hang on! I've just been reading mummy's email, it said they CAN rule me out and it wasn't me at all your honour and I don't have any love sprogs at all! Phew.

Oh I need a lie down after all that excitement.
I'll write soon.
Love Timothy. xxxx

20th June 2016
Day 83

My name is Timothy Conehead the Invincible and I'm a border collie, it has been a week since my last confession and Sir Macca gets to share my birthday with me!

Hello, there have been some major incidents to report your honour and I  am a birthday boy.

So well there we were halfway through the prepared menu and the juices were flowing beautifully but then there is always one fly hovering like a suicide bomber waiting to jump into your ointment and anyway we've got lots more fish to fry on pot and opium and all kinds.

It's a shame really as mummy was going to let me set up a standing order and send money to help but you can't win them all in a big city and anyway the camels not a bit happy again and some people need to understand that without praise and gratitude the cheese goes off the boil never to be grated again and if all you ever do is criticise you'll never get anywhere in life.

So anyway when you have your menu all planned and the roast confit of lamb has to turn into a peeking duck with no warning even the coolest chef might end up doing a Gordon Ramsey and not being very flocking happy with some flocking people and just pick up their bed and walk.

It really is a good job I'm here to keep all the spirits happy or maybe that should say to go to the shops to buy more spirits so we can all be happy? I'm not sure now because drowning is never really a good idea because nobody really prospers from it and anyway you can't get any money back on the bottles anymore.

So where was I?  Oh yes pickled again, no I was just reporting in about the three major incidents your honour and none of them were my fault either. Well I suppose one of them might have been my fault but I put it to you that you're not pinning the other two on me.

Firstly Sir Lord Jack who is expected to live forever collapsed and I'm sure it was nothing to do with me knocking him over last week and anyway I haven't even looked at him sideways since mummy gave me the death stare and threatened to toast my eyeballs for supper if I did. He is fully recovered now and doing well with the little nip of gin he gets with his breakfast of poached mackerel or

Angus Aberdeen mince every morning.

So I was still wearing my blinkers and then everything was settling down to what is considered normal in this place of correction and our Freya collapsed and we almost had to have an air ambulance brought in for her and the SAS were on standby to shoot me unconscious ready to stand trial on a date to be pulled out of a hat. Thank goodness she came around in time and all is well now, I have promised to try to look very hard to look where I am running in future and to not use my sexy body as a battering ram your grace.

So then just when I thought I could have a rest and go and play with myself Laddie the Baddie who has trained me well in all things naughty, was going bazonkers at our nice postman who I think is still called Les and likes me a lot and takes no notice of any of us as we all try to round him up. So while Laddie was trying to disarm Les from his letters he just collapsed and he is only about 18 months younger or less than Sir Lord Jack who can do no wrong. Mummy was frantic but I helped her to give Laddie the kiss of life and he is back to normal now, I say normal but we think he has a few butties missing from his picnic box but then I'm not really sure that mummy can be classed as normal either but don't let her know that I told you otherwise it will be “Curtains for you young Conehead' and that's for sure!”

Oh I nearly forgot to tell you because of all this flocking upset that has been going on I have had my very first birthday! I share my birthday with Sir Macca of Beatleland [that's another name for Liverpool in case you wool's didn't know.] I hope Sir Macca realises how lucky he is to share his birthday with me, I think I will write to him to check that he knows. Mummy gave me an extra crust with my dinner to celebrate and she let me smell Sir Lord Jacks Rib-eye steak too, I am such a lucky boy and Freya let me sit on her her head too!

I had a lovely picture taken with me and His Eminence which shows clearly we are Superglue our bones together. No that's not right, we are in the boneyard making glue. No Sir Lord Jack is 007 and I'm Oddjob. No Freya Jack and Laddie have all rolled their eyes at me now and I'm all confused, I know it was something to do with glue. I know!! We have been having some bonding sessions and I'm not allowed to look at him sideways in case I come unstuck!!

I will report back in as soon as I can.
Love Timothy xxxx

Wednesday 1th July 2015

My name is Timothy and I'm a border collie and surprise surprise I'm in trouble again!It has been ten days since my last confession.

Hello,
I'm going to be sent to jail for false accounting and misleading the

public and if I'm very lucky I will be incarcerated and then be let out early for good behavior. When I told you about how poorly Sir Lord Jack was and how sad I was well I may have jumped the machetes and javekins because he is proving to be a phenomenon. We are not sure what has happened but we think the tramadol giving him proper proper sleep has perked him up and his appetite is better too. The honey flavoured loxicom that lives very high up on a shelf nowhere near the Beatles albums that takes you to meet the green llamas and the giant daffodils and the friendly strawberries has sorted the muscles out in his legs and we are sure the bach flower remedies added to everything helps too but most of all we think it is the naked dancing at midnight around the Magic Tree that's done it.

It could maybe just be the power of Love though.

We are hoping to have a long happy summer together and Sir Lord Jack is going to tell me everything I need to know if I am ever going to become wise as he is and as I'm desperate to taste the Aberdeen Angus steak mince, the freshly cooked gammon joint and the poached haddock I am going to listen very carefully.
I will of course keep you posted.
Love Timothy xxxx

t

Monday 6th July 2015

My name is Timothy Conehead the Invincible and I'm a Border Collie, it has been nearly five days since my last confession.

I'm sorry I have been failing in my duties to keep you up to date on my corrections but I have been really busy looking after the

Golden Oldies.

Sir Lord Jack of the Kingdom of Love is going to need a zimmer frame soon. He is a very sprightly golden oldie who has suddenly realised he is 17 and eligible for a free mobility car. He has an enlarged heart and also a heart murmur and at night he is in pain and tosses and turns a lot and it is making us all very tired.

Nobody got much sleep last night because of it so we have been to see Uli, the vet who thinks I am lovely and is in love with me. Well she says we are not to give up yet and we have got some more medicine for tonight so as we can all get a good nights sleep and not be moaning in the morning because moaning isn't good at all for anyone.

So anyway I'm busy trying to be good and not too sexy although that part is difficult and I'm trying to understand that red hot pokers are not toys and it “is not the done thing Conehead to remove a plant from its pot so you can drink the water in the pot underneath!”
I'm not doing very well really your honour and there are a few more camels in the cellar and I'm not sure how many and I'm not saying how many times I've put myself in the naughty drawer!

Anyway so anyway we are all about to have a nip of gin and a valium and a fag and that will calm us all down apparently, erm no I've got that wrong. Sir Lord Jack says we're going to meditate not medicate but we may medicate tomorrow if we get no sleep tonight. Meditation is very good for you apparently and mummy is often to be found in a trance-like state but Laddie says that could be the spirits. I didn't know we had any spirits, nobody tells me anything around here you know.
I will keep you all updated on our sleeping patterns and thank you to everyone for all your good wishes.

Love Timothy xxxxx

Wednesday 8th July 2015

My name is Timothy Conehead the invincible and I am a border collie, it has been two days since my last confession and I am a druggy.

Oh it's just terrible news, there has been a catsupatree and I have

been incarcerated in the vets for 22 years for drugs offences your honour.
So it was like this Sir Lord Jack has been put on some drugs for his arthritis and we are being neglected while mummy is upstairs trying to tempt the eminent one down for his fine dining experience.
So well anyway, while this tempting was taking place and without prejudice your highness we were being neglected and having to cook our own breakfast and everything and there was this special cooked ham in the ham cupboard that tastes really nice and it was beckoning me to have a taste and so I did and it was delicious and so I ate some more because it just kept beckoning me to and it wasn't my fault.

So anyway mummy has a friend and he is a pirate and he dresses up in sexy ladies clothes and he buys this Aldi's special ham for his troll dog who is called Jazz and is very pretty not like her daddy. I've got my eye on Jazz only if the pirate catches me I might be hanging from his yardarm in bits while he drinks his rum and feeds me to the albatross.

So where was I anyway oh yes, so you see I was being seduced by this Aldi's special ham from the ham cupboard and then I found the drugs and they did smell really nice and there was a Taste of Honey which made me think of the Beatles and soon I was singing.. 'For the benefit of Mr Kite there will be a show tonight on trampolining' and then I was just dreaming of the fun I could have on the trampolines and I was having so much fun with the giant daffodils, the green llamas and the purple strawberries that came to play with me and I was just having so much fun and there was even a hole in my shoe and Neil was just going to sing to me when all my dreams were shattered.
“AARRRGGHHH Conehead!! What have you done now!!”

It was mummy and I don't think she was very happy and there I was in a ceremony and being thrown into the back of the chariot like a dead parrot with no thought for my shattered dream or anything and I was rushed at high speed , being careful not to go through any red lights or do anything else illegal for fear of having to attend any courses your honour. The high speed rush ended at the vets and I thought I might see my sweetheart Uli but she wasn't on duty so I had to make do with Paul who makes me sick. No, no I mean he gave me medicine to make me sick and all my lovely best special ham from the ham cupboard was removed forcibly from me by projectile vomiting. Paul said as I was obviously a hardened druggy I had to be incarcerated for 24 years. I would be fed poison kidneys as my punishment! Mr Dunn who loves rescued border collies would have been kinder to me for sure but he was on holiday but his lovely daughter Lisa was there and she was kind to me but then she said her dad would have told me off more!!

So anyway, the good news is I have been let out early for good behavior and mummy said to tell you that the tramdol that Sir Lord Jack has been having for his night pain is beginning to work and he managed to sleep until four this morning before the heart murmur came back and woke everyone up. Everyone except me of course because I was still being incarcerated in the vets against my free will and being fed poisoned kidneys. Paul, the one with the poison kidneys has given mummy some more medicine for Sir Lord Jack that is to be kept on a very high shelf away from the Beatles Songs so that Jack can sleep longer and his murmuring heart can rest more and everyone can have beauty sleep, because we all need it except me as I am just so handsome.
Love Timothy. xxxx
P.S. I enclose a picture of me incarcerated at said vets, I wanted a red bowl to go with my red collar and my red heart name tag.

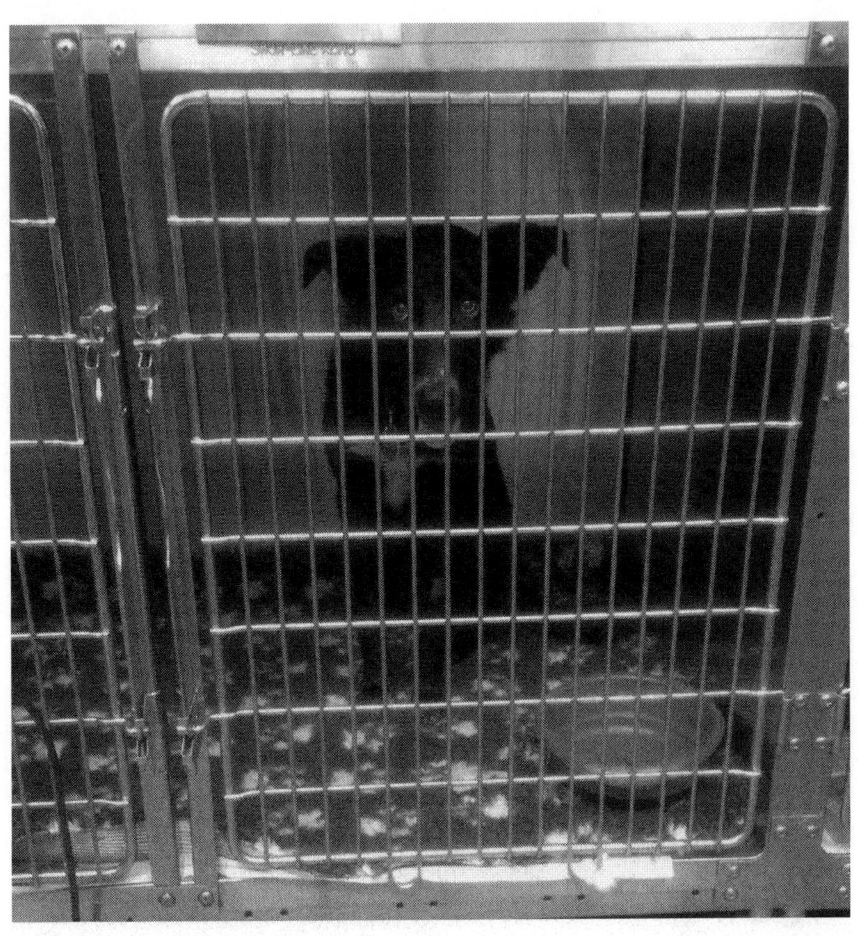

❤

Thursday 9th July 2015

My name is Timothy Conehead the Invincible and I am still a border collie. It has been one day since my last confession and there has been a miracle at Love House.

Hello everybody, we think someone broke in last night and swapped Sir Lord Jack for a younger version who just looks exactly the same but is fitter!

So well you see it was like this mummy came home from work last night and threw some scraps at us cheaply fed dogs and then she fed His Eminence with a tin of oily fish which is good for the heart and he didn't save us any he ate the whole lot! Mummy was so pleased and we all went for a walk .

So anyway he had his tramadol from the very high shelf that is nowhere near where the Beatles albums are and I haven't managed to climb yet and then we went to bed. The thing is you see your honour that when the alarm went off at 6:06 in the morning we were all gobsmacked and dead pleased as the heart murmur never came to wake us up or anything not once. Sir Lord Jack slept the whole night through.
And so the thing is we were sent downstairs to do our chores and get our breakfast of bread and water ready and clean the grate out and fetch the coal while mummy needed to do some enticing with golden balls but then suddenly she didn't need to because Sir Lord Jack just decided to get up by himself and come downstairs 'just like that' and we think he must have been dreaming about Tommy Cooper and he was smiling.

So then when we were starving and begging for our rations mummy did cook His Lordship his Aberdeen steak mince and when she was hand feeding him he decided he liked it so much and he liked it a lot and then he turned into a wolf and it was all gone before you could say bunnie testicle and there was just none left and so the mummy gave him some more and the wolf appeared again and so it was gone!! Then he demanded to go on a walk and while he was out he even had a little run.

Mummy thinks he must have been in such pain from the murmurs in the night and no sleep that he must have been exhausted when he woke up and that is why he had no appetite for fine dining but now he is wolf man and I know he had some more Angus Aberdeen mince when we got back from a message because mummy took him in first and they were a long time and it did smell really tasty when us poorly fed dogs were allowed in but there was no food left out for us.

I will write again soon.
Love Timothy xxxx

## Friday 10th July 2015

My name is Timothy Conehead the Invincible and I'm a border Collie. Just 24 hours have slowly passed since my last confession and mummy is not flocking happy again.

Hello everyone, well you see it was like this. Mummy was playing with herself on the intersex and ordering more things to arrive in plain brown paper parcels from the postman who thinks I'm really handsome and is called Les.

So you see I kind of sauntered off in a very sexy way as only I can and then snook into the room where The Beatles live in their albums along with The Birdie song and The Bucket of Water song and Lulu's I'm a Tiger and lots of other rare and iconic music. So while I was being currently unsupervised I just kind of thought if I just see if I can stretch up there again I might just get me another fix because I was missing the green llamas and the giant daffodils and the friendly strawberries and so I thought 'I know if I just stand on the Bach flower remedy wooden box on my tip toes I might just be able to reach the nice drugs.' So well anyway I couldn't and that's that your honour but I did manage to get the hyperdermic plunger thingy and it tasted so nice so I did try and eat that instead. I was enjoying myself only mummy heard me crunching the plastic and appeared like a ghost from A Christmas Carol and she did give me the deathly death stare and she wasn't a bit flocking happy your honour and so she did sentence me to be passed through the mincing machine 27 times then fed to the dead camels and then to be on bread and water for life or at least until then end of the week. I am pleading for leniency here and also for any spare drugs anyone may have to send to me please in plain brown paper parcels. Les is used to them now and won't ask any questions.

Love Timothy xxxx

P.S. Sir Lord Jack has had poached haddock and milky weetbix for breakfast after a good nights sleep and he did wake us all up at 5 am but that was ok and he enjoyed his 40 minute walk this morning too. We were allowed to watch him eating his poached haddock and were promised the bones but it turns out it had been filleted so we just had to make do with scraps again. We are all just honoured to be allowed to watch.

Saturday 11th July 2015

My name is Timothy Conehead the Invincible, Super Conehead to my friends and I'm a border collie. It has been one day since my last confession and I'm having some psychological testing.

Hello everyone, I'm being very good today because mummy says if she keeps calling me a naughty boy then I will soon become a sulphur filling pot of tea so if she keeps telling me what a good boy I am then that is what might happen. So anyway I am reporting that Sir Lord Jack had his best night so far last night and we all had sweet dreams except mummy who was drowning in a sulphur filling pot of tea until Super Conehead the Invincible came to the rescue and so I did rescue her but I don't remember because I was having fun with the green llamas and some sexy little border collie chicks but I don't mind taking the credit.

I wonder if this means I'll get fed today. So anyway where was I? Oh yes his Highness. Well he didn't need enticing down this morning and he came down to a sumptuous breakfast of creamy weetbix followed by Angus Aberdeen mince cooked over a low light with carrots julienne and diced leek. Us poorly fed dogs were thrown the vegetable peelings and told to clean up the mess if we wanted to go for a walk. So we did your honor.

We had a nice walk and met some grandchildren again so we decided to be grandchildren tested once more just to make sure we all passed again and we did. Mummy who had kept on walking with the Chosen One while we played with the grandchildren was feeling sad and one of the grandchildren followed mummy and started talking to her. He told her that he used to have a dog who looked a lot like Sir Lord Jack and he was called Fletch and then he told mummy all about another dog he had that was called Jess. Mummy let the little boy have a cuddle with His Highness and thanked the him for sharing his memories with her because they had made her smile again. Did you know we had a great Nan? Well we do but she is in the Land of the Light and her name is Jessie Fletcher and that is why the little boys memories made mummy smile because it must mean that Little Nanny Fletcher is with us in spirit.

I wonder if that means mummy will have a special port tonight or a brandy? Mummy is drawing some pictures today for her next unicorn book so I'm going to be playing with myself on the intersex and I'm going to see if I can crack the code to her playful account to see what interesting things I can buy.
I will write soon.
Love Timothy xxxx

Friday 17th July 2015.

My name is Timothy Conehead the Invincible and I'm a border collie. It has been almost a week since my last confession and apparently life is a series of beginnings and endings and I'm about to be recycled.

Hello,
Oh no! I'm in trouble again and I don't know what to do. You see I was just minding my own business and playing with myself on the intersex and then I was talking to a pirate and I might just have just maybe but only maybe suggested that mummy had a special lettuce plant your honour and it was only a joke and I would never let anyone see it or anything. Everyone knows anyway that it's good to grow your own and more healthy for you as there are no added chemicals like LSD or anything and there are no E numbers added and I was only trying to help as I thought I might sell some and get mummy a little couple of bob to buy Sir Lord Jack some more fine dining experiences and it's all gone to pot and I'm going to be recycled and everything and I don't know what to do as I was only trying to help.

Did you know that mushrooms need an even temperature of 16C or 50F to ensure good healthy growth? Mushrooms, mushrooms, who said mushrooms it wasn't me, honest I've never been near the mushroom cellar and there is no magic carried out there at all whatsoever your honour honestly.

The sprinkler system is top of the range and the heat lamps are too, I think the heat lamps are for keeping food hot at dinner parties but I'm not sure what the sprinkler system is for. Mummy says she is calling the hangman in if she catches me laundering anymore secrets on here. 'It'll be the noose for you young Conehead or if you push me too far it will be for me!' Oh no!!

Apparently some people have been upset about my tales but I can promise you that I love my mummy and no part of Timothy, that's sexy little me have been harmed in the writings of these diaries.
I will write again as soon as I can.

Love Timothy xxxx

❤

Tuesday 11th August 2015.

My name is Timothy Conehead the Invincible and I'm a border collie, it has been about three weeks since my last confession and Sir Lord Jack has been signed up by Munchen glad back!! Oh erm no he is a Megalomaniac! Hmmm, apparently that's not right either, I know! He is a Misogynist!! Oh flipping flocking heck that's still wrong!! I know I'll ask Princess Freya she seems to know everything round here, bear with me..

Hello everyone,
Life is very hectic here, there are still several chickens running around with no heads but not as many as last week! Sir Lord Jack of the Kingdom of Goodness and Love is enjoying visiting Rob Dunn who is his special vet with the Jedi laser training machine that he said perhaps he had Munchhausen's but he was only joking! Us mere mortals think he is a celebrity as all the staff have to come and say hello to him on his bi weekly visits and have to have a stroke and a cuddle and a little chat with him. I'd quite like that myself but I can't reach any medicine to overdose on so I guess I'll have to wait until I am as old as His Highness, sigh……

Anyway so anyway where was I? Oh yes we had the munchies but don't tell anyone and we were all chilling and medicating and dreaming about green llamas and then His Highness woke us up again….. The cold laser therapy has almost sorted his arthritic pain out but now his heart is waking him up and making him pant heavily again..
The bad news is that Mr Dunn has said the lord is going into heart failure but the good news is that we can now have heart medicine that will double his life span!! Er no

what I mean is that if he had four months to stay with us now he will have eight months of fine dining experiences!! So now he is on an Ace Inhibitor, I'm not sure if that means he won't be able to play poker again but I'll let you know…
Princess Freya keeps busy doing the housework for mummy and Laddie the Baddie helps me to make a mess and keeps showing me new ways and mummy hasn't been arrested for a while.

Life is good and I will write again soon.
Love Timothy.xxxx
I'm attaching a picture of His Highness on his way home from Jedi training today. He has his own personal dream catcher. We have to share one.

Wednesday 19th August 2015

My name is Timothy Conehead the Invincible and I'm a border collie mummy it has been about a week since my last confession and I have been surfing on a dating site....

Well you see it was like this your honour mummy was just thinking it was about time she had someone to mow the lawn and cut the hedges and the house could do with decorating again and so she had a word with me and she went like this, she went "Conehead come here young man" and so I did and then she went like this " want you to look for a handyman for me please on the intersex and stay away from sites that sell adult toys, we've got half a dozen boxes full of them in the herb cellar already we don't need anymore!!"

So anyway there I was and I was just thinking 'now where would you go to to find a gardener and a decorator?' so I thought 'I know a nods as good as a wink to a deaf bat on a helter skelter' Before anyone knew a thing I was on a dating site, I just thought if I could find someone nice for mummy then she might be more busy with seeing to him that she might not notice me quite so often and so I did.

His name was Mick with a nice picture and he looked dead fit and young but was just a bit younger than mummy and he was 6ft 2inches tall and slim, the best bit was that he liked dogs too. I sent him some messages and mummy's mobile phone number and she agreed to meet him!

He wanted to meet all the family and so we met him near where we walk and we were all excited and everything. He didn't look like his picture though, was wasn't a bit slim, he wasn't a bit slim at all and he wore glasses that were not in the picture and had had a bath in aftershave!

Anyway, we met him in our chariot and showed him where we walked and sent him there while we drove back and came out of our back gate and walked across the fields to meet him again. Freya kept bringing him the ball to throw but he couldn't bend down to pick it up, then he told mummy he was waiting for a second hip replacement and should have brought his stick with him. Mummy rolled her eyes at me and Sir Lord Jack didn't look too happy either, '"his isn't the sort of gardener I ordered Timothy" she whispered hysterically as she gave me that instant death look of hers. I think she was hoping for some scrumpy pumpy as her battery supply has run out.

So where was I? Oh yes, so you see we got taken home and not so nifty Mick was sent back across the fields to find his car and the postcode for the meeting place where he was buying lunch for mummy.

Not Nifty Mick keeps his figure trim it seems by eating 20 ounce stegosaurus steaks it seems and he ordered a 12 ounce one for mummy which was good as she brought half of it home to share with us. After his banquet Not so Nifty Mick who had said he had the occasional social cigarette lit up and then proceeded to chain smoke. I don't think mummy will be seeing him again..
Mummy says she will do the hedges and the lawn herself and the decorating can wait. I don't think she was very happy.
I'll write again soon.
Love Timothy. xxxx

Thursday 3$^{rd}$ September 2015

My name is Timothy Conehead the Invincible and I am a border collie, it has been more than two weeks since my last confession and I am here to report an encounter I had whilst climbing..

Hello so you see it was like this your honour, mummy had disappeared somewhere and I was being unsupervised and so I thought "I know , I'll see if I can have some fun" and so I did.

There was this box you see and it just happened to be next to the big pine unit that is called 'The Bar' I think the special reserve port that I like lives in there. I know I've seen mummy getting it out from there. So anyway I thought "I know I'll just climb on this box and see how high I can get and see if I can find any drugs or anything else nice to have" and so I just climbed up and I could see this packet of biscuits and they did look very nice so I decided to just have one lick just to check and was sure that would be ok so I did.

Mmmm the lick was nice, it was kind of chocolaty but not quite chocolate and it was just creamy but not cream and mmmm so I just accidentally ate one of them and oh it was superb and nice at the same time and so I found myself accidentally eating all of them and just as I accidentally finished the last one mummy came downstairs and she caught me hook line and sinker and I couldn't even pretend it wasn't me your honour. I was immediately whipped into a frenzy and grounded in the mushroom cellar with twelve months hard labour and 'm not allowed to play on my skateboard or play with my friend Max the big German Shepherd or anything. So just for now I'm sat on the driveway hoping that the nice postman whose name I can't remember called Les brings mummy some plain brown paper parcels to make mummy smile again so she forgets to banish me to the cellar after lunch.

I'll bet she moves that big brown box now too.

I'll try to write again soon,I promise.

Love Timothy. xxxx

P.S. Just to let you know that Sir Lord Jack still rules the roost here and we have to wait on him hand and paw. Xxx

❤

26th February 2016

My name is Timothy Conehead the Invincible and I'm a border collie. It has been nearly five months since my last confession.

Hello everyone,  I'm very sorry I haven't been posting for a while but I have just been so busy running around after Sir Lord Jack of the Kingdom of Golden Balls!!His Eminence is on about eight or nine different types of medicine and it takes me all of my time just to remember which one to give him and when.

He is a pherenome and continues to enjoy his twice weekly visits for Jedi laser treatment with his personal vet Mr Rob Dunn. I think everyone has heard about Sir Lord Jack and his amazing longevity helped by the laser therapy and everyone who meets him thinks he is marvelous. We think he is pretty marvelous too, well he has marvelous meals that's for sure.

Anyway I've been told that I have to come on here today and apologise for eating one of mummy's friends birthday presents.

It wasn't my fault really, mummy left it on the breakfast bar and went to work and it was calling to me. I was very strong for a while but the calling got stronger and stronger and it just defeated me and so well anyway it just called once too often and that was it! I was mesmerised by the singing and I was seduced by the ferrero rochers and they were just delicious and I might put them on my birthday list and I'm very sorry Aunty Pauline and when I get my pocket money for cleaning out the moat I will buy you some more and promise not to be seduced by them again, at least not until next time. It would have been perfect if mummy had left the port on there too....

I hope you have a lovely birthday Aunty Pauline

Love Timothy.. xxxx❤

P.S. I am enclosing a special family photograph we all had taken, it wasn't easy but we did it! Adam P. Johns is a star.

This is Princess Freya, Laddie the Baddie, Sir Lord Jack and Timothy Conehead, that's me oh and mummy in one of her many red jackets.

Shower Reactions

Saturday 11th June 2016
Day 73

My name is Timothy and I'm a border collie. It has been nearly three months since my last confession. Today is a very special day indeed.
Hello everyone, I think I have written more diaries but I may have mislaid them due to all the stress of looking after the golden oldies. Today is one of the most special days ever recorded in time! You see not that many border collies get to be 18 years old but Sir Lord Jack of the Kingdom of Goodness and Love is 18 years old today. He got birthday cards and lots of messages in all the different groups and he got a very special cake with 18 on it.

When we got up in the morning mummy made him an extra special breakfast before we went on our walk he ate lots of it too. When we got back he opened all his cards and presents and then he decided to have a little nap.

In the afternoon we all went on a very special message and we went to Sir Lord Jacks favourite spot in the Pinewoods, oh it was lovely. The poorly fed ones, that's me and Freya and Laddie in case you didn't know had to be on our best behaviour and on our leads too. His Eminence was allowed to wander around off lead, mummy said he is a free spirit I think he is a spoilt brat but don't let mummy know I said that. We found a nice place to sit and we had a lovely picnic. I say lovely and it was but what I really mean is that Sir Lord Jack had another fine dining experience in the woods with best steak and profiteroles and the poorly fed ones got spam! To be fair your honour we were really grateful for that spam, bread and water can play havoc with your bowels if you don't get anything else thrown in from time to time.
Quite a few people spotted us and came over to watch us having our party and they all thought we were dead cool, especially me. We got a red bowl to share to drink our water from but golden balls just drank out of mummy's water bottle. I'm going to learn how to drink out of a water bottle when I grow up..
It was really lovely and an honour to be in attendance to His Majesty on such a salubrious occasion.

I will try really hard to keep up my diaries.
Love Timothy. Xxxx

P.S, I am enclosing a picture of His Eminence with his 18th Birthday cake. Isn't he a handsome chap and looking fabulous for his age?

❤

.

18th June 2016

## Day 80

My name is Timothy Conehead the Invincible and I'm a Border Collie. It has been five days since my last confession.

Hello, I just needed to let you know how I was getting on in Kathleen's House of Correction. I am here to be corrected your honour and anyway it has still not worked and I'm still on a months trial, on the first day of every month I have to attend a meeting in front of the committee your honour and apparently when I have been good for a whole month then mummy might adopt me!

I do try very hard to be good and mummy is always saying that I am very trying so I must be doing something right.

So anyway where was I? Oh I remember being corrected. Well you see because I am taking so long to be corrected I have to go to borstal too and wait till you hear this. Sir Lord Jack of the Kingdom of Goodness and Love who can do no wrong used to go to borstal too! Can you believe that? His Eminence in borstal? He told me so himself. When he arrived he was a lot wilder than me so mummy had to take him to borstal and he was dead good and won prizes and he learned how to dance too! Well that's what he tells me.. He even still has his dancing stick that he used to touch and follow. He won prizes too, I wonder if I will win any prizes....?

Anyway today is my birthday and apparently I share it with another special person called Sir Macca I don't think he had to go to borstal but he has won lots and lots of prizes and mummy hopes his good fortune will rub off on me because we share the same birthday. I'm not sure if that means I'm going to meet him though so I can rub up to him?

I had to go to borstal today even though I should have been having a birthday party or a day out in the pinewoods like Sir Jack had last week. Anyway Aunty Rita wished me happy birthday and said I was dead boss with the heel work and looking gorgeous and sexy of course.

So anyway listen, I'm not supposed to know this but I think me and

His Eminence are going to see Sir Walter Rally, erm no that's not right, no I've got it we're going to see Woody! No that's not right either but we are going somewhere special right after borstal tomorrow and I have heard that my special personal trainer Andrea is going to be restraining me at borstal tomorrow as well as Monday! I'm not at all sure about whether that is because I have been very good or very not good.
I've just been told we are going to Woodvale to see The West Lancs Dog Display Team in action, just me and his eminence.

I'm going in a minute because I am not supposed to be playing with myself on the intersex but I just wanted you to know that I have been allowed back out of the mushroom cellar and that I did get a cake for my birthday today so I must have been good at something at some point.

I promise I will try to keep up my diaries again if I can fit it in with all the other chores I have to do.

Love Timothy xxxx

4th July 2016

Hello my name is Timothy Conehead the Invincible and I'm a border collie it has been two weeks since my last confession.

Oh it is just terrible here, I'm rushed off my feet looking after the golden oldies I'm on a nursing course specialising in caring for elderly collies who have wobbly head syndrome otherwise known as too many gins in the vestibule it is and also ones who have a heart so full of love that they are struggling as they don't want to leave their mummy. You should see all the medication I have had to learn about and Sir Lord Jack also gets lasered twice a week too for his chronic arthritis. I hope when I get old there is a young whippet snapping around and looking after me.! When mummy goes to work I spend all that time learning all the important things I need to know about learning to be a top notch border collie. Sir Lord Jack rolls his eyes around a lot while he is teaching me and he says I need a few more buttys adding to my picnic but that I'm not nearly as bad as wobbly head aka Laddie the Baddie! His Eminence used to go to training school and is giving me tips on how to be teachers pet and everything.

Anyway, there has been a dicky rectum and I've heard mummy talking on the phone about it and apparently if Boris Trumps then all the excitement will hit the fan and there will be fall-outs everywhere! There's a Blair witch hunt because he is still hiding his Weapons of Mass Debation and the last thing we need is for the Eagle to land on the Common.

Oh it's all very worrying and now the Conman is standing down and so is the Garage and guess what? I heard mummy saying that if we are not careful it will be Timothy running the country! I am just so worried, I can't do everything, I'm busy doing my nursing degree and looking after the golden oldies and I have to look after the plants in the cellar and clean the moat out once a month too. I really just don't have the time to run the country as well.

I'm going to leave you with a picture of me in my nurses outfit, now don't worry I always look like I'm badly done to but actually I like dressing up especially in my nurses uniform. Mummy says it's called a fetish but I am sure it's called a nurses uniform.
Love Timothy. xxxx x

Sunday 17th July 2016

My name is Timothy Conehead the Invincible and I'm a Border Collie. It has been two weeks since my last confession. I've got terrible news, our Freya has been grounded for life!

It was like this your honour and nothing to do with me and I'm not prejudiced or jaundiced or anything. We are very lucky you see and where we live with mummy in her house of correction being corrected we have lots and lots of land behind us and we can run and run and run and we do and it's fab. It was great last year and we had fun hiding in the wheat fields but this year they are growing oil and well you see Freya likes having adventures in there with the foxes and the bunnies oh and the pheasants and partridge and everything! She takes me with her sometimes and it's a bit scary but fun too and I always make her come back to mummy. The problem arose your honour when she decided to go on her own and forgot to come back, twice!! A nice lady called Wendy from borstal brought her back in the morning and then later on that same day she did it again and mummy had to take Sir Lord Jack back home and we had a search party of me and Laddie and Max and his dad and we all looked for her and we looked until we had sex on our eyes and still we couldn't find her and so we all had to go home because it was too dark. I kept disappearing too but I didn't want mummy to worry about me so every so often I would just pop out and wave in a very handsome way.

We all had to go home to bed but mummy was really worried and so she just cat napped but I don't know whose cat she used because I don't think we have one anymore unless it lives in the cellar with the camel with the broken back. I'll have a look next time I water the herbs down there. So anyway where was I? I know in the cellar watering the, oh no silly me! So anyway mummy kept coming to see if Freya had come home yet, every half hour and guess what time she came in? Go on guess?? It was 2:30am and mummy was so pleased and not pleased too but mostly pleased but not with Freya's muddy paws! Max's dad thinks she must have got trapped in one of the ditches and that's where we will look if it ever happens again.

I don't think it might happen again though because Freya is not allowed out now unless she is chained to mummy! She nearly pulls mummy over sometimes too as she tries to run to round up the bunnies with me. Freya is getting used to being imprisoned on a lead but she is happier now that the orange training lead has been replaced with a red one so as everything matches and is red. Mummy thinks this corporal punishment might just remind Freya that she is with us and not an illusive butterfly.

I'll let you know how her training goes.

Love Timothy xx

Friday 5th August 2015

One of the saddest days in my whole life and I know many of you will feel the pain of losing a precious soul. I share with you my eulogy to Sir Lord Jack of the Kingdom of Goodness and Love, I . hope you don't mind.

***On a beautiful sunny day in the year 2000 Sir Lord Jack bounced into my life and it would never be the same again. Today I have had to say goodbye to him and reluctantly let him go and my life is so much richer for the Love we shared and never will be the same again.***

***The staff at Freshfields Animal Rescue Centre, the rescue centre that Mr Dunn my vet has supported for his entire career, said he was 2 years + when I adopted him and to reach the magnificent age of 18+ is truly wonderful, two more of my collies reached seventeen but Jack wanted to stay longer.***

***To say he was a handful is no exaggeration. He was wild, a street dog who had been rounded up by the rescue centre on the south side of Liverpool. He wanted to run and run he did. Many times my heart would be thumping as I walked with my thirteen year old Basil on Formby beach and failed to get Jack to respond to my calls, he was far too busy chasing gulls to notice that the tide had come in around him! He would have to swim to get to shore and my heart could settle once more. He loved to chase the crows and they used to wind him up too, letting Jack chase them to the top of a sand dune and as he got closer flying off sideways, thankfully Jack didn't follow that lead and would race away looking for another crow or some gulls to round up.***

***My boy wasn't interested in toys, he occasionally destroyed the odd squeaky toy but really he preferred to just run and round up anything he could, birds, dogs, me. He liked rounding things up***

*and reading all the wee mail and of course leaving suitable replies! I have pictures of Jack sat next to rabbits after he had round them up. He never harmed a single one. The other things he liked was to play hide and seeks around the house which I've always played with my lot, it's good fun especially if you have bunk beds and they can't figure out where you are in the room. The other thing Jack loved was playing footsie with me. It was like playing snap, he would just appear and put one of his feet on top of mine, I would laugh and put my other foot on top of his, he would pull his foot out and put it on top once more laughing all the time!*

*Jack was not easy, he was super hyper, collies are hyper anyway but Jack had also been a street dog which I assumed made him super hyper. I very nearly gave up on him but I am not a quitter.*

*Quitters never win - winners never quit.*

*I found a training school in Halsall and we started a twelve week training course where Jack became a superstar. I hadn't had any formal dog training before, I had just read books and watched some videos. This was good stuff and I was taught how to understand Jack and how to teach him to train me or the other way round if I was lucky. We continued with the training beyond those twelve weeks until they were forced to close because of personal difficulties. Jack was trained now though and would do anything I wanted him to do, We became so close. to the point that I could bring Jack to me by moving my eyes a certain way and if I mouthed 'I Love you' his tail would wag. I taught him to jump through hoops, to sit on my knee and to jump into my arms and we had a training stick that Jack could follow as we learned some heel work to music.*

*Not too long after training finished my Basil died and as I came out of the vets with just Basil's collar and lead Jack was busy bouncing around the car, I showed him Basil's lead and his head dropped and he went and sat in the back of the car and never moved once all the way home. He comforted me in my grief and we became closer still.*

*The little pip squeak, the once wild street dog became my Top Dog that day and remained Top Dog until he passed. He knew he was number one too and thrived on it, always first in the pecking order for whatever was going. I doubt he would have been a top dog in the wild, he was far too gentle for that and just about everyone tried to topple him but I always reinstated him, he was my Top Dog and no one was going to change that.*

*The Love that shone from out of his eyes was amazing. We grew closer still.*

*We went to a local training school to do agility and Jack loved it, he could jump through hoops of fire and was fearless. We were asked if we would like to join their display team training group but in then end we couldn't as I went down with carbon monoxide poisoning from my own gas fire.*

*During Jacks stay with me he survived quite a few collies who came to be 'corrected' Basil, Scampi, Lady, Tipper, Christie, Monty and the very beautiful and complex Jessica. He went grey very quickly when she arrived. He has been my comfort for each and every passing and each time we grew closer still. He was gentle with everyone and everything even his food, he did everything with gentleness as we all should.*

*When Timothy arrived last year I had never intended to keep him but although he looks nothing like him his ways, his personality, his excited barking when out, his mischievousness, his looking badly treated look all remind me so much of my young pip squeak and so I couldn't let him go.*

*In the past all of my previous collies have been diagnosed with something and then were gone very quickly but Jack is no ordinary collie.*

*This time in 2015 Jack became ill and was diagnosed with chronic arthritis and I knew he had an enlarged heart along with a heart murmur and it was confirmed that he was now in heart failure. I was of course devastated. I expected him to have days to live. Thankfully Mr Dunn and modern medicine had other ideas and Jack was put onto powerful drugs for his heart, he also had diuretics and painkillers, water tablets and an ace inhibitor to counteract the heart medicine, His chronic arthritis was brought under control by a cold laser therapy machine, the only one in the northwest or at least was at the time.*

*Amazingly Jack could run again and my dearest boy had had his life extended. Jack was so funny or should I say clever, he went off his food and so I tried him on other things and he ended up being better fed than me. He really learned how to play me and I knew what he was doing and let him, He got to the point were he wouldn't entertain dog food and his diet consisted of braised steak, steamed chicken breast, sausages, gammon, mackerel, cod, fresh salmon, sardines in oil, [Mr Dunn had once said that oily fish was good for the heart to I got as many as I could down him] , Oh, Aberdeen Angus mince was one of his favourites too! I've never allowed a dog to be picky before, this is your food eat it or it gets binned was always my way, but Jack was different and it amused me no end to experience his likes and dislikes.*

*His final two weeks meals were sirloin steak, rib-eye both cooked medium rare, lambs liver and cream cakes and ice cream.*

*Our visits to the vet were twice weekly and he knew the drill. We would go in and he would drag me past Lisa or Sarah on reception who would say hello to him and tell him to go through. He would be looking for Rob as he went and when he got to the scales he would climb onto them and stand there looking at me and waiting for me to say ok. I don't know what he thought he was doing but he knew that's what we did and so he did it. His weight fluctuated from 16+ kilos to 18+ so we had to keep an eye on it. We would then go back to the waiting room where he would try to open Robs door and when he couldn't he would stand with his nose pressed to the part that would open and wait.*

*The others in the waiting room used to be amazed to see a dog who couldn't wait to see the vet but as I explained to them how beneficial the laser therapy was and how Jack clearly knew it was helping him, they could see why. The vet nurse Helen used the laser room from time to time and the look on Jacks face if she was in there was hysterical. Give Helen her due, not only did she always say hello to him but when she was caught in there she would also apologise to him for using his room. Thank you Helen. Priceless.*

*Mr Rob Dunn is the best vet ever and I could never have asked for a kinder or more compassionate vet. Jack preferred Rob and on one occasion the lovely Uli did his laser and Jack didn't want to go home as he hadn't seen Rob! Jack used to nuzzle into Robs arm while he was doing his shoulders, he loved Rob and the laser.*

*Love and gratitude is everything in this life and last year I began to be grateful for a fabulous summer together and when we got that I focused on him still being fit and happy by 4th October [the feast day of St Francis of Assisi the patron saint of animals. ]*

***then I focused on Christmas, Easter, my birthday, Jacks 18th and am so grateful that I got to love him and keep him with me for all of this. I knew this was his last summer, none of us can live forever and as much as I was hoping for the whole summer with him again I could see he was getting tired..***

***Jacks beautiful smiles are what I will miss most he was such a happy boy, playing footsie with him which he did right up until the end and his inimitable hugs. He gave the best hugs I have ever experienced, really pushing his head in on me and I am lucky enough that it was captured two or three times on camera. Oh and they way he would often hold my hand when posing for photographs.*** ☮♥ ❤

***All my collies, fifteen I think now, have all been rescues and some more damaged than others. I have loved each and everyone of them but I adore Sir Jack, He was my right hand man, my mate, my top dog, my comforter, my Joy. I'm sure he had a human gene, Mr Dunn agreed with this. We were joined at the hip.***

***I imagine Jack escaped from his original home because they didn't take him out. I would never have been allowed to get away with not going out. He reminded me several times a day it was nearly time for more walkies and he would plonk himself down next to my car at some point and demand to be taken out 'on a message' Every single day I took him out on 'a message' and if I had nowhere I needed to go I would just take him fro a drive. He had me hen pecked really but he was funny with it.***

***My boy tried his very best to live forever and amazed myself, friends and the vets at how he just kept bouncing back, how stoic he was. The past two weeks I could see him slowing down and on Monday Jack asked me to let him go. It breaks my heart but it is***

*cruel to let someone suffer needlessly so today I let him go to be with the other eleven already waiting for me at Rainbow Bridge.*

*Jack and I were joined by an invisible elasticated chord and I know he will still walk behind me when I go walking.*

*This morning just me and Jack went on a very 'special message' to the pinewoods, his face lit up when he saw where we were, he has always loved it there. So we walked and talked and had rib-eye steak and profiteroles and talked about Rainbow Bridge and how time goes very quickly there and it won't seem like a long time until I join him. We hugged and then we went to see Rob and we had our laser therapy as usual and then we said goodbye. All things must pass.*

*Today I celebrate the life of Sir Lord Jack and give thanks for the privilege of sharing sixteen years of his life with him, for his Love, his loyalty, his gentleness, his mischievousness, his friendship and for the honour of nursing him this past twelve months which meant we grew even closer. Until we meet again my special boy I will miss you every minute and I promise that when we do meet again and after we've kissed and cuddled the first thing I will do is to take you on a message and you can hold my hand again.* ☮❤

*R.I.P. Sir Lord Jack* ❤

Jacks passing is just about the hardest loss I have ever experienced and mourned but life must go on. I was lucky to find him and I was lucky to find that I had so much love and support from friends and from people I had never met who had followed Sir Lord Jacks adventures long before Timothy became his grasshopper. I was touched to hear that so many people across the globe had cried when Jack passed, they had come to love him too along with our daft tales. I was deeply touched by almost one hundred messages that were added to the eulogy I posted and then by cards, texts and messages and flowers that arrived over the following few weeks. I will always be grateful to all of you, you have my heartfelt thanks.

❤

It took me almost six weeks before I could get myself back into training with Timothy. I didn't want his diaries to end with Jacks passing either but I knew I would have to let Timothy announce it in his own inimitable way. It took me two months before I could bring myself to do this though.

Saturday 5th October 2016.

Hello My name is Timothy Conehead The Invincible and I'm a Border Collie. It has been two months since my last confession and the news is terrible, Sir Lord Jack of the Kingdom of Goodness and Love has passed his sell-by date and has popped his clogs. He is currently swinging the lead somewhere over the rainbow and waiting for mummy to take him on a message.

Oh dear, it had to happen but our Jack really didn't want to leave mummy but apparently we all have a sell-by date even mummy has one!
It has been really sad here as she cries a lot because she is sad that golden balls has gone belly up and kicked the bucket. She keeps thinking she see's him and she talks to me and she goes like this "Where's my Jack Conehead?" and I go and look for him but I can't find him anywhere! I keep looking as I want to smell rib-eye steak again. One day mummy asked me where he was and I looked up above her head because I could see him there smiling away as usual, I think mummy knew I could see him because she cried and gave me a big hug.

I wish he could come back though because the food here has got worse, we are the cheaply fed dogs but at least we sometimes got the leftovers from Sir Jacks fine dining experiences but now we just get bread and water and the odd rabbit that we have to catch for ourselves out on the Haven!

Have I told you about the Haven yet,? Well you see there were just a few bunnies once but now these bunnies have been erm copulating and I think they've been copulating rather a lot!
I think copulation is a good thing really and I'd like to copulate a lot with our Freya or with anyone basically, I wonder do they have

dating sites on the intersex for handsome black collies looking to copulate..? If more of us copulated more often then there would be more love in the world and less stress, oh and your spots on your face might go too if you have any in the first place.

Anyway where was I? Oh yes I know copulating!! Erm no, there are bunnies everywhere for us to herd but the thing is someone must have told the buzzards because now there are loads and loads and loads and at least three of them coming over all the time for bunny snacks and if me and Freya disturb them then we get the carrion without having to work for it!

Since the oil fields have been harvested Princess Freya keeps discovering other places to hide in and bunny island is one of her favourite places, I don't think mummy is very pleased and I heard her telling her friend that she is going to buy a cow bell to put around her neck so she knows which bit of wilderness she is hiding in!

Anyway, just so as you know I'm not lying if you look for me on YouTube you might find the video of me and my friends Duke and Ruby oh and Uncle Chris who loves me and gives me treats just because I am adorable, handsome and awesome. Duke caught the bunny and he let me have a lucky rabbits foot.

The very best thing about the video is that it made mummy laugh so much, I hope we have another bunny party on the Haven very soon. I like it when mummy laughs a lot.

Love Timothy. xx ❤

Tuesday 18$^{th}$ October 2016

My name is Timothy Conehead the Invincible and I'm a border collie. It has been about two weeks since my last confession and I'm in big trouble again.

Hello, mummy was very cross with me after my last confession, she went like this, she went 'Conehead come here right now, how dare you be so irreverent about Sir Lord Jack telling people he had gone belly up and was brown bread , have you no sensitivity? I just sat there looking handsome and gorgeous but it didn't work this time. I'll have to ask our Freya if she has seen my sensitivity lying around anywhere. I didn't know he had been ordained, when did that happen? Nobody tells me anything. He is probably being shot out of a holy cannon as I plead and grovel and will be Saint Sir Lord Jack by the time I've cleaned the moat out again.

Anyway let me tell you about my ongoing correctional training. Oh it's just awful the things I am forced to go through here. The first time I did the agility course the seesaw tried to kill me and I was traumatised. Mummy said it was just one of those things and because it wasn't successful in killing me that it would make me stronger and so mummy did take me back and so the next time it was really windy and a big lorry went passed and made a big loud sound like a bomb to blow me up with and it scared me more. The seesaw just kept banging and banging and banging and I knew it still wanted to kill me and the horse in the next field stuck his head over the fence and laughed at me and I just didn't want to go back ever again. So mummy sat me in her nice comfy chair and she cuddled me and she did talk to me and she told me again that the seesaw was an accident and accidents happen so you can get stronger and fight them back next time, she said the lorry with the bombs was just someone sending me good luck wishes and she said the horse wasn't laughing it was just telling me I would be OK if I just kept trying. So I went back.

My Aunty Rita who adores me because I am just so sexy and handsome and adorable helped me lots and lots and lots and she has nice sweeties for me too and she likes cuddles and we did some lessons in the middle of the torture course with the offending seesaw just yards away your honour and looking at me in a very sinister and threatening way. I wasn't on my lead so sometimes I ran off but neither mummy or aunty Rita followed me so I had to come back into the valley of torture or I wouldn't get any sweeties. Aunty Andrea makes me work really hard on our Monday lessons and right next to the deathly seesaw trap and I have to think so hard with my mind that I haven't got room for thinking about the possible consequences of it noticing me there.

Lat week the lovely Sharon, who might be another aunty said no one is allowed to use the offending seesaw until I have been decapitated and I was just so relieved but the she invited me into the ring of torture once more, oh it was terrible but she was putting sausage on the dog-walk and did try to entice me onto it your honour and I wouldn't. I could just manage to reach over and get it without actually touching the wood, then she sat on it with her feet either side and called me to her and I thought 'Oh she must need a cuddle like mummy so I threw my arms around her neck and gave her a big big cuddle. Everyone was laughing especially the new people who were being shown around but I just knew that Sharon was enjoying the big cuddles I was giving her. After our cuddles I did a few of the jumps too and it wasn't quite as bad as last time and the seesaw never said a word.

Anyway the next day it was raining and we did most of our lesson in the polygamy tunnel and I was just so cool., I did most of the things that mummy ordered me to do and when it was time for the torture course Sharon was there again and I could see she was pleased to see me and so I was really good and got all four feet on the dog-walk, everyone seemed really pleased about this so I jumped most of the jumps and did a bit of weaving and then I saw the A-frame and I decided to be invincible and just flew over it! Like a Boss!

Everyone looked happy and apparently if I carry on being decapitated bit by bit each week  then the valley of torture could turn into something I might even enjoy. Oh I can't wait to tell my aunty Rita how brave I've been and see if she has forgotten to send me any sweeties.  Sir Lord Jack would be so proud of me.  Freya and Laddie are laughing at me, apparently I am being desenitised and not decapitated well anyway they both begin with D and one of them is happening to me.

I will keep you informed.
Love Timothy xxxx
s

Sunday 23rd October 2016.

My name is Timothy Conehead the Invincible and I'm a border collie. It has been one week since my last confession.

Did you know I had to wear a straight jacket? I'll bet you didn't, you have no idea what I have to endure here day in and day out and it has got worse since golden balls ascended to The Bridge. The worse thing about it is that it is pink. Pink! I mean I am the invincible adored by millions and feared by many and she puts me in in a pink straight jacket. Pink. Luka laughs at me when he sees me and even Luna does and she can't even see! Erm I may have got that ever so slightly wrong, our Freya tells me that Luna who owns Lynn and is a white wolf is erm a bit deaf. She still laughs at me. The straight jacket is allegedly part of the slow decapitation training process.

This week I was mostly good and mostly did everything I was commanded to do by the commander! That's mummy in case you didn't know and apart from the first ten minutes on Saturday I was just dead boss like. If you don't know what 'dead boss' means then you must be a wool or a woolly back and not come from Liverpool. Dead boss means awesome, amazing, magnificent, outstanding and marvelous. We have a unicorn called Sparkle and she makes boss lentil soup.

Anyway you have perverted me from my story you woolly backs now where was I? Oh I know torture training. So anyway after being mostly dead boss for the first part of the lesson including jumping through hoops and weaving through hoops which was really fairly painless and quite fun, it was time to enter the ring of terror and jump things that needed jumping.

This wasn't the normal ring of terror, this was The West Lancs

Canine Centre professional display team torture course! All of the others in my class all took their turn and they seemed to like it.

Then it was my turn..

I ran through  a dark tunnel and jumped some unsuspecting jumps and then Sharon talked me into going up the professional dog display dog-walk. Have you seen how high it is? Have you seen how long ot is? Would you do it? I didn't think so.

Well the lovely Sharon who thinks I'm dead cute and handsome enticed me up to the top your honour but when I got there I could see the top of Snowdon and I went whoa! I said no way mourinho and like Boston Bob in the 2016 Grand National who pulled up at Bechers Brook, I pulled up and refused to move until my solicitors arrived. I had to be air lifted out but after a half time pep talk from Sharon and a quick bribe from mummy I was sent to finish the rest of the course. And was able to complete most of it.

I did eventually escape and found my Aunty Rita waiting outside to give me some cuddles and tell me how brave I was.

Sunday passed without incident your honour and I even jumped fences and did the A-frame in the ring of torture course and guess what? I ran through one of the tunnels without having to have Sharon hold my hand  or a bribe from the commander. My Aunty Rita wasn't waiting for me today, she must have forgotten to smell the Rosemary or should that be coffee?

I'm looking forward to going to the concentration camp tomorrow to see my Aunty Andrea.
I will try to report back soon.
Love Timothy xxxx
P.S I am enclosing exhibit A a photograph where X marks the spot and I am being awesome with everyone else doing a down, this also shows clearly Luna the white wolf laughing at me. Xx

❤

Sunday 6th November 2016.

Hello my name is Timothy Conehead the Invincible and I'm a border collie. It has been nearly two weeks since my last confession and I've been Sabbaticaled!!!

Baa baa black sheep have you any wool? Yes sir yes sir three bags full. One for the master one for the dame and one for little Timothy who lives down the lane!
I do live down the lane you know and I'm black Just like the sheep and I'm a sheepdog too! I'm not a wool though I'm a Liverpudlian and full of Scouse!

I had to do more torture training last weekend again. Auntie Rita was there and i was really pleased to see her again and she gave me some sweeties for turning up! She took us straight into the ring of torture though and I had to be enticed in with bribes. We all had to do a down for an hour with the offending seesaw watching my every move, I was doing really really well until Lynn who is owned by Luna the white wolf made a rude noise and I thought it was the seesaw coming at me with a machete! I was out of that down as quick as Mick the Miller came out of trap six at White City Stadium to win the grey hound derby. I was as white as a sheet and shaking in my boots but mummy told me it was ok and put me straight back into the down and bribed me again so I stayed there a bit longer. Mummy said I did really really well and that I'd soon be decapitated if we just carried on working hard each week.

Sunday wasn't so good though your honour and I think someone forgot to tell the offending psychotic seesaw with murderous tendencies that I was back in the room and needing some peace and quiet because it just banged and banged and banged away like it was angry or maybe it had a hangover like mummy sometimes does, only don't tell her i told you or I'll be thrown into the mushroom cellar again for life!

This evil peace of equipment upset me so much your honour that mummy wrote me a sick note so I could be excused Mondays lessons with Auntie Andrea. The lovely Sharon is looking into ways of handicapping the aforementioned tormentor by slowing it down and making it resist me or silencing it altogether.

I have now been sabbaticled until further notice or at least until the Saturday the 12th whichever comes first! It's Becky's birthday weekend so I'm needed here anyway to serve the food and drinks.

My hands won't be idle, oh no I am undergoing wobbly wood training as apparently I have to accept that wobbly wooden things are not all out to get me. The big piece of wood was supplied by Wendy who is owned by Ben and Ruby. I try my very best to fly over it but I am not managing that very well, if I walk on it I get a treat. If I sit on it I get two treats! I was going to jump the wall which would have been easy until it suddenly got coned off courtesy of June who is owned by Misty and Shayla. I am currently working on a 0 - 60 from a stop so as I hardly touch the wobbly wood at all, if a Lamborghini can do it then so can I!

Mummy says the wobbly wood is staying forever and ever or until I walk slowly over it like a Boss!

If you look on YouTube you may just find a short clip of this home torture I am being forced to do your honour as evidence, it shows quite clearly the wobbly wood and also the offending cones.

I will write again soon,
Love Timothy. xx ❤□

Sunday 13th November 2016
Remembrance Sunday.

My name is Timothy Conehead the Invincible and I'm a border collie. It has been one week since my last confession and Sharon has super powers!!

Guess what? When i went to torture training this week I found that Super Sharon who is owned by Wilma and Helga who are the a double act and perfect in the display team, had cornered the killer seesaw and she did man handle it onto it's side so it couldn't move! Apparently she went like this she went 'You just stay down there on your side you killer seesaw where you can't look at him and stop upsetting Timothy Conehead! You are ordered to stay on your side until Timothy [that's me] has been totally decapitated and is over the nervous breakdown you gave him when he didn't even ask for it!'

Oh I was so pleased to see it handcuffed to the ground and so I wasn't scared in the ring of torture and I jumped some super high jumps when they weren't expecting me to and I did everything else except the dog-walk from nemesis. I believe it is in league with the killer seesaw your honour and do not trust it at all. My Aunty Rita was there when I finished and gave me a treat for being so clever.

Anyway the next day was Remembrance Sunday and my granddad who I haven't met because he lives in the Land of the Light, well you see he was a Royal Marine in the second world war and so is Super Sharon's son. They are the Elite in Her Majesty's forces and very special people join it. Apparently my granddad who wasn't well known for being a diplomat used to say things like 'Those Yanks have marines and a navy we have Royal Marines the Royal Navy and they are the real men and they are the Elite. He served on H.M.S. Bulolo and he served in Burma and Singapore and he met Lord Mountbatten of Burma and had his picture taken with him too. The Royal Marines motto is ' Per mare per terram' which means by sea by land. I wonder if we learn swimming at The West Lancs Canine Centre, I'll have to ask Super Sharon. Her dad was in the Royal Navy and he got lots of medals and an extra medal this week from Costco! No that's not right, our Freya just rolled her eyes at me but she is only jealous, the medal was sent from France but it went to the wrong address by mistake which was Costco and everyone is very proud of him and his name is Joseph Carter,

So anyway you see mummy wasn't sure about taking me torture training again today but she did and was glad because everyone observed the two minutes silence in honour of all the brave people and animals who fought to save us, those who died and those who came back home. Everyone was silent even me because mummy kept my mouth enticed with sausage in case I decided to have a chat with anyone,

Now what was I going to tell you next oh yes I was mostly fabulous in being obedient especially being sent away to lie on my mat. I often wonder why mummy just doesn't leave me at home if she keeps wanting to send me away but I like to humour her otherwise I get locked in the mushroom cellar for months at a time.

Go on guess what else? Well I bet you can't, go on just have a guess.

So, with the offending aforementioned killer seesaw disabled and handcuffed to the ground I set off in the ring of torture agility course. I jumped jumps and ran through tunnels and mummy couldn't keep up with me so I just did the A frame by myself. Like a Boss! The last piece of equipment was the dog-walk your honour and I hesitated and then I thought about all this wobbly wood training I've been forced to do Anyway, I was feeling really confident and Super Sharon was there with better treats than mummy has and so I went to have a look and before I knew I had been enticed to the top and even though mummy nearly ruined it all by nearly tripping over the bottom part of it I just carried on because I could and I was enjoying being enticed by Sharon's special treats and before I knew it I was back down the other side and everyone was cheering and everything and I just felt like a Boss. It was like Istanbul all over again.

Ben's human Wendy gave me a treat and Lynn who is owned by Luna gave me big hugs when she heard how good I'd been.

All the way home mummy kept telling me how clever I was and she might even add some sausage to my bread and water dinner later. I wonder what I have to do to get fine dining like Sir Lord Jack...
I promise to write again as soon as I can.
Love Timothy. xxxx

P.S. I am enclosing a picture of my granddad and also his medals. His name is Victor Harry Ashcroft and he was a very proud Royal Marine. ❤

22nd November 2016.

My name is Timothy Conhead the Invincible and I'm a border collie. It has been one week since my last confession. I think washing mummy's dishes should be done with my ear defenders on.

One potato two potato three potato four, I'm just laying her playing with myself, it's really quite pleasurable you know and can be quite orgasmic at times. You should try it, it's fun to hold your plums ask Billy Butler he was always doing it with Wally. I'm told it's good for your skin and it gives you lovely shiny hair. five potato six potato seven potato more...

I'm down here in the mushroom cellar playing with myself because mummy had a wobbler. Oh yes she did, there was steam coming out of her ears and a foreign language was coming out of her mouth. I was shocked your honour, deeply shocked.

I was just cleaning as many dishes for her as i could find, I think that's why she keeps us you know, so it's less for her to do. So there I was and being Invincible and I know not to surf the kitchen tops, "surfing is for when we move down south to catch some waves and surfing is for finding toys and things on the intersex Conehead" I've been having this drilled into my head with a pneumatic drill everyday since I've been here.
Where was I? One of you has perverted me when I wasn't looking, hmm, it'll be one of you woolly backs for sure. Oh I know, playing with myself..
So there I was being Mr Cool on cleaning duties and I could just see the Stilton enticing me to come and look at it. It hasn't enticed me for a long time your honour not since the last time I was hung drawn and quartered. But there it was soliloquizing like nobodies business and it was soliloquizing straight at me and I just thought and I just

wondered that as the responsible adult was nowhere to be seen and because I was being seduced by the mellifluous soliloquy of the said Stilton I could just feel myself being bewitched and mesmerised and I tried so hard to resist and then I tried even harder and then I just went of 'oh fluff it' just like that and I ate it. It was lovely and creamy just like the last piece I was bewitched by.

To be fair your honour I didn't touch the bottle of port she had opened to breathe or the rib-eye steak that was hoping to be dressed in that very fine Stilton. It was just a moment of weakness, it's really hard trying to survive on bread and water when we have to work so hard.

I've got ten years to reflect on that 'fluff it' decision, ten years hard labour. I might never be awesome again.
I will write again soon, if I survive..

Love Timothy xxxx

# ABOUT THE AUTHOR

Timothy Conehead has an honorary degree from Liverpool John Moore's University and was shortlisted for the Nobel Peace Prize for Illiteracy in 2016. He is friends with the Liver Birds, coaches Sir Ken Dodd's Diddy men in the art of nonsense on Friday mornings and has agreed to be interviewed by his mate John Bishop in his new series to be screened later next year. He adores Craig Charles and is set to partner Danny John-Jules in the next series of Red Dwarf. He is a frequent visitor to Anfield and it is rumoured that he is currently in talks with Jurgen Klopp and could be the Reds secret weapon in the New Year. It has also just been confirmed that he will feature on Sir Paul McCartney's latest CD in 2017.

Only joking!!

Timothy is really clever and intelligent and needed a ghost writer to help him and so Sir Lord Jack of the Kingdom of Goodness and Love came back from Rainbow Bridge to help him when mummy was at work but he couldn't do it all and so we threw a bag of flour over mummy and put a white sheet over her so she could do some ghostly writing for me too! He has written to Santa Claus to ask for a new seesaw that will be kind to him and his dearest wish is to meet Paul O'Grady and to visit his farm to help him to round up his six sheep.

In between doing ghostly writing for me and taking me to torture training mummy also is a hypnotherapist in the posh street in Liverpool just near the red light district where we think she plays games for money but we are not sure your honour they could be mind games or they could be any sort of games but I think she is on top of her game or on top in the game, I'm not sure now. She tells everyone she is a professional though and a nod is as good as a wink to a blind camel hiding in the cellar.

Mummy also writes about our unicorns and there is a series called 'Life on Belles Haven' and the unicorns are good and not naughty or anything and they are all for children but grown-ups like them too. Mummy writes lots of poetry I think it helps her to feel calm after trying to train me and saves her from needing therapy

I am enclosing exhibit A your honour A a picture of my ghost writers, mummy with Sir Lord Jack. Mummy loved him more than love itself and I know His Eminence felt the same way, he didn't want to leave and I know he waits patiently at The Bridge for mummy to take him on a message but I want her here with me for as long as she can because we all love her too. We used to be The Fab Four and now we are The three Musketeers.

Mummy is also known as Kathleen Phythian but only when she answers the phone and then she goes like this, she goes " Kathleen Phythian how can I help you?" and then she talks to people about all her problems, no sorry she talks to people about their problems and then when she comes off the phone she is mummy again!

Sometimes she is called K.P. nuts but please don't tell anyone I told you that or I'll be hung drawn and quartered again and sent to clean the moat out followed by the slammer for me in this life, the next life and however many other lives I have to live your honour!

Thank you for reading my book, I hope it made you smile and remember,

All you need is Love

and a border collie or two or three or four or more.....

Love,
Timothy Conehead the Invincible!

It is all you need....

❤

Exhibit A

Sir Lord Jack and Mummy.
Forever In Love.

**If you are looking for fun inspirational and motivational books for your little ones, why not have a look at the 'Life on Belles Haven' series. These are all written and illustrated by Kathleen and can be found in a number of libraries and on Amazon.**

❤

**The Candyfloss Tree.**

**Unicorn Bridge.**

**A Tale of Two Unicorns.**

**Sparkle the Unicorn.**

**Twinkle the Unicorn.**

**Ruby the Christmas Unicorn.**

**Coming soon:-**

**Starburst the Unicorn.**

**Moonbeam the Unicorn.**

❤

Printed in Great Britain
by Amazon